TEMPTING THE COWBOY

A PAINT RIVER RANCH BOOK

ELIZABETH OTTO

Entangled Publishing, LLC
2614 South Timberline Road
Suite 109
Fort Collins, CO 80525
Visit our website at www.entangledpublishing.com.

Indulgence is an imprint of Entangled Publishing, LLC.

Edited by Danielle Poiesz and Guillian Helm
Cover design by Kelley York

Manufactured in the United States of America

First Edition October 2013

To Matt. For twenty years of believing in me.

Chapter One

Rylan Fredrickson looked at the mass of beer-chasing cow-boys crammed inside the small, dark bar, reaching instinctively for the reassurance of the gun she no longer kept at her waist. This hole-in-the-wall couldn't possibly be what her therapist, Dawn, had in mind when she'd told Rylan to stop rocking her ass in the corner, step out her front door, and start experiencing new things.

Just breathe, Rylan, and let life happen.

She'd stepped out her front door, all right, and straight down a testosterone-and-beer-fueled rabbit hole. She was supposed to take the bus from Madison, Wisconsin, to Greenbrook, Montana, where a ride to Paint River Ranch would be waiting for her. Not fearing for her life on the threshold of a horror-movie-worthy bar called The Reaper. "Experience new things" was starting to look like a fail. If Dawn weren't also her best friend, Rylan would have strangled her hard and slow for the shitty life advice.

Dawn's "let life happen" mantra was supposed to help heal Rylan's emotional wounds. But so far she'd spent twenty-four hours on a packed Greyhound with broken air-conditioning and then gotten dumped at a run-down gas station slash bus stop. The bucktoothed station attendant broke the great news to her that she'd gotten off in the wrong town. Paint River Ranch was twenty minutes away, and to add fuel to her fire, no one answered when she'd repeatedly hit the ranch's number on her cell phone's speed dial. Life was happening, all right, and it wasn't doing much to make her feel better.

From the moment she'd answered Paint River's online help-wanted ad to when she'd sold everything but the clothes and few mementos in her travel bag and hopped on the bus, she'd been second-guessing the sanity of taking this leap. She was interviewed over the phone and hired via e-mail for crying out loud. What had she been thinking?

Escape. A clean, far, far away escape from the ache in her heart and the emptiness that never went away, that's what. Rylan hugged herself and took a deep breath to steady her nerves. She'd been a cop in one of the busiest college towns in the country. Making this journey shouldn't have her so undone. But the sun was setting behind the mountains and soon she'd be stranded in a town the size of a postage stamp. Undone was too light an expression.

"Suck it up, Buttercup," Rylan muttered as she drew a big breath through her nose, hitched her duffel bag over her shoulder, and crossed the threshold. The beat of a Little Big Town song blasted in her ears. Surveying the interior, Rylan spotted the bar across the room behind several scattered tables. Her nerves jacked; she'd have to cut through a mass of drunken men to reach it. The memory flashed in her mind—the sound of gunfire, searing pain, blood on her hands.

Rolling her shoulders back and standing tall, Rylan smoothed the front of her jeans with sweaty palms before weaving through the room. Chatter paused. Cowboys turned to look her way with halfhearted interest. She stomped down her unease at having so many eyes on her, and let out a relieved huff when conversation and the sounds of drinking and cards being shuffled started up again as quickly as they'd paused. *Shake it off*, she chastised herself. *This is a different place, a different bar.* After six years in law enforcement, it was hard to forget that not every man in every bar was packing a weapon, just waiting to put a bullet in her.

Once bitten and all that.

A baritone voice wafted by as she approached the bar. "Help you, young lady?"

Rylan glanced around but couldn't see the source.

"Down here."

She followed the tones and blushed to see a very short person whose forehead cleared the bar by only the fraction of an inch. How that huge voice came from such a small man, she had no idea.

"I'm sorry." Rylan gaped. "I didn't see you there."

"Statement of my life." The man stepped up onto a stool and grabbed a tumbler from the rack. "What'll ya have?" He was balding, with a ring of chestnut-and-gray-peppered hair, the top of his head dotted with age spots.

"A ride?" Rylan asked. The bartender stopped halfway to getting a napkin with the rise of one bushy eyebrow.

"With these stumpy legs of mine, that's not a request *I* personally get very often." He winked and set a napkin in front of her. Rylan laughed.

"The gas station guy said I might find someone heading to Greenbrook in…" A loud boom upstairs cut her off, and the floor above shook with violent boot stomps. The bartender sighed, shaking his head. No one else seemed to mind or notice. Rylan glanced over to see a door at the top of the stairs open. Voices and laughter rang out from behind it, and a man clomped unsteadily down the staircase.

"Dammit, Cole! You lost. Get your drunk ass home!" a voice from upstairs shouted a second before a hat flew down the staircase after the man.

The bartender sighed again as the upstairs door slammed. "Poker game going on." He pointed with one finger to upper level. "So, where exactly are you headed?"

"Paint River Ranch," Rylan said, eyeing the cowboy as he slapped his hat against his thigh before attempting to settle it on his head. The hat fell off. He snatched it and tried again, completely missing this time. Glossy black hair curled around his ears and the nape of his neck. A dark T-shirt hugged his broad torso, the one arm Rylan could see defined with smooth, bulging biceps as he put the hat back on. A warm flush settled in her chest. Drunk or not, if he was this sexy from across the room, how hot was he up close? Rylan's brow furrowed at the thought. Yeah, that's what she needed to be thinking about right now.

The bartender gave an enthusiastic guffaw. "No kidding." He pulled a tap of beer and held it to her. "Drink up. You're going to need it."

Rylan accepted the glass with a questioning look. "Why's that?"

The bartender nodded to the cowboy who swayed his

way around a row of tables. "'Cause that's your ride."

She'd survived being shot, a couple car chases, and the swine flu. There was no way in hell Rylan was getting tangled up with a six-foot-plus, drunk-ass cowboy. Sexy or not.

"Why exactly is he my ride?" Rylan crumpled a bar napkin in her palm while watching the cowboy stagger through the crowd. Somehow, he maneuvered his tall, lean body against the far end of the bar, hip jutting out with one leg cocked as though he had all the time in the world. She half expected him to fall over...and was slightly disappointed when he didn't.

"He's Cole Haywood."

The name had a ring of familiarity to it. "So?"

"*Haywood*, as in *the* Haywoods of Paint River Ranch."

Rylan clenched her eyes shut. *Oh, shit.* Maeve Haywood had been her contact at the ranch, the one to conduct her phone interview. If her brain weren't so tired from this disaster of a day, Rylan would have made the connection right away.

Time to get her intel straight. "So, he's the...?"

"Oldest son. Co-owner."

She rolled her eyes. "Right." *And technically my freaking boss! Great. Add drunk, hot boss to the list of surprises today.*

She'd been hired as the executive housekeeper—a fancy title for cleaning lady—but it didn't matter. She'd wanted a simple job, an escape from the rigors of being a police officer and the constant cycle of misery she couldn't seem to pull herself out of. When Maeve had offered her the job, Rylan had eagerly accepted. She'd do laundry and clean toilets until her fingers bled if it would help ease the empty feeling in her chest. Fourteen months hiding away in her house, trying to deal with debilitating grief and crushing lawsuits, had led to this. A huge change. A fresh start.

The bartender slid a new napkin next to her glass. "There are three Haywood boys—Cole, Tucker, and Levi. They run the ranch, along with their mama, Maeve. Mr. Haywood died last year, and since then, you could say...well, things ain't been the same. Cole isn't a drinker, for instance. And he's a wasted sombitch right now." He smiled wide when Rylan raised her brows. "Come on now," he chided. "You don't seem like the type of woman I need to mince words around. Am I right?"

"No mincing," Rylan confirmed, wiping condensation from her glass with a flick of her thumb. She might be a woman, but she was harder than most, and it showed. Her demeanor and the way she carried herself equaled all cop and no nonsense. Feelings and emotions? Nicely tucked away, thank you very much. She both loved and hated that part of herself, knowing that the rough parts of her former career, and especially her life, had taken some of her softness away.

"So you're telling me *that* intoxicated cowboy is my best hope of getting to Paint River Ranch tonight?"

The bartender gave a sympathetic shrug. "Yep. And you'd better catch him before he starts drinking again."

He indicated that he'd watch her bag as she slipped off the stool with a hissed expletive. *This ought to be fun.*

"What's his normal? You know—happy drunk, mean drunk, gotta-tase-him type?"

The short man hunched his shoulders and winked. "I've never seen him drunk before, so you tell me when you find out."

"Great." Rylan frowned. The place seemed louder all of a sudden. Or maybe that was the blood rushing in her ears. Sounds banged in her head, her heart thumping painfully as she started toward Cole. The closer she got, the more the nerves tore up her insides. The crowded bar was making her cop Spidey-senses go off—that was all.

When she slipped into an opening between Cole and the man next to him, all her senses went haywire, calling bullshit to her theory.

Cole leaned his elbows on the bar, his profile to her. Tan skin, slight stubble on his square jaw, one perfect curl of black hair peeking from beneath his hat. Close-up Cole was so much better than faraway Cole.

Rylan cleared her throat, more to get a grip on herself than to get his attention. "Mr. Haywood?"

Cole glanced at her, tipping his beat-up hat back a little to rest his eyes on hers. Rylan's mouth went dry, from nerves, fatigue, or whatever was making her brain swirl. Cole Haywood had a delectable lower lip and a top one that curled up just a bit, making him look inviting and sexy as sin. His eyes just had to be the brightest turquoise she'd ever seen, too. They were brilliant, even in the dim light.

"Yes, ma'am?" The muscles in his arms flexed as he braced one hand on the bar. Her skin heated, and a teasing ache stabbed her right between the legs, making her jolt a little, her right hand shooting out to grab the bar in response.

Mortified but holding it in like a pro—at least, she hoped she was—Rylan let go of the bar and offered him her hand. "I'm Rylan Fredrickson."

Cole's eyes lowered to her hand, but he didn't take it. His gaze made a slow ascent, up over her chest—paused there—then moved to her face and settled on her lips as a half-grin decorated his own. She smirked at his appraisal. At least *she'd* been covert in checking him out. He wasn't even trying to hide it.

"Ah… Is this a conversation we should have, you know, in private?" The wicked glint in his very blue-green eyes made her insides squirm. Her mind went wayward for a second to all the sweet possibilities "private" might entertain with a man this gorgeous before her rational self bitch-slapped that thought into next week.

"No!" Her lip curled. "*Definitely* not."

"So you're not coming on to me?" He hitched a finger at the female bartender, and she promptly placed a beer in his hand.

Rylan rubbed her forehead and took a steadying breath. "I have no clue why you'd think that, but considering you're my boss, Mr. Haywood, that would be highly inappropriate."

The guy behind her choked on his drink with a snicker. Cole's eyes went wide. "What?"

Rylan spread her hands. "The new executive housekeeper? That's me, and apparently, you're my ride to the ranch, so—" She should probably ditch the sarcasm, but he was drunk, so they were even.

"What the hell?" He turned to fully face her, grumbling something about a man not even being able to get drunk without work interrupting. His tight shirt dipped into the lines of his chest, creating a tempting outline of firm pecs, narrow waist, and tight abdomen. A thick leather belt with a square silver buckle set the tone for the snug, well-worn jeans clinging to his long legs. Rylan hitched an eyebrow. At least there was one good thing about this trip—the hype about cowboys being sexy as hell was true.

More than a little irritated with how her lust was playing tennis with itself, Rylan crossed her arms. "Hell is appropriate, actually. Now down the drink, and give me your keys." She had one hand on her hip—habit, she supposed, from reaching for cop toys to make jerks like Haywood behave. His eyes fell to her lips again and stayed there.

"You were supposed to take the bus to Greenbrook. *Tomorrow*." His tone implied she was an idiot.

Irritation growing.

"Right, well, sometimes things just don't work out the way they're supposed to."

Like life.

His hand cupped the beer glass while he studied her. Rylan stared right back, wishing the butterflies would take a hike. What was this reaction about? Cooped up too long with too little interaction with the outside world, she guessed. Her body was reacting to the first enticing man she'd seen in too damn long. Good thing Cole was her boss so she wouldn't be tempted to act on her brain's internal "look at the pretty cowboy" jumping and pointing.

Cole pulled his lower lip between his teeth and narrowed his eyes. "You're a little ornery." He reached one hand to her shoulder and flipped a chunk of her hair.

Rylan's breath ran away as the back of his hand brushed over her collarbone. A shiver raced over her body, warm and sweet. She leaned away from him. "Excuse me?"

He shrugged, a slow smile crossing his face at her reaction. "That's okay. Ornery is good."

Her lips parted to sling an insult, but she refrained. No sense in wasting perfectly good angst on a drunk who wouldn't remember it in five seconds. "I'll play along. *Why* is that good?"

Cole took a slow breath, his eyes darkening. "Because you're pretty. I like pretty. But I don't like ornery. So we should be just fine." He nodded as though he'd just made a deal with himself and was quite pleased about it. Before she could even think of a response, he shoved his beer away, untouched, and moved from the bar.

"Let's go." He dug in his pocket, produced a key and some cash. He threw the cash on the bar and turned to walk away. Still mulling over his words, Rylan grabbed his wrist on instinct.

"You're not driving." She put her hand out for his keys.

He scoffed and shook his head, words a bit slurred. "Boss, remember?"

Rylan pursed her lips. "I can see the headlines now: *Paint River Owner Cole Haywood Kills Employee in Alcohol-Related Crash*. Goes to, oh, I don't know, *prison* for vehicular manslaughter." Rylan swallowed hard. Drunk driving was something she'd had enough of over the years—more than. The offense hadn't just been a daily part of her life as a police officer; it had ripped through her personal life like a meat grinder on steroids.

His nostrils flared like he was trying to hold back a laugh. "You're not driving my truck."

Since first impressions had already gone right out the window, she was okay with expressing herself. If it got her fired, so what? She'd figure something out. Let life happen, right?

She gave a resolute nod. "That's fine. I don't need this job that bad. Thanks anyway, Mr. Haywood." Rylan turned back where the short bartender was watching her things. There was no backup plan, but sleeping in the alley was preferable to getting into a truck with him driving. She'd made it four steps when Cole's strong hand gripped her shoulder. Shocks raced down her spine as his warm fingers pressed into her flesh.

"Dammit, woman. Fine." He spun her around fast. She tipped forward right into him. Her heart short-circuited, her breath stalled in the single moment her chest made contact with his. With a gasp, she put her palms on his hard body and shoved herself back. He grabbed her left wrist with one hand and flipped it over. His thumb made a soft back-and-forth sweep over the pulse point before he dropped a set of keys into her palm with the other.

His eyes were blocked by a shadow cast by the brim of his hat, but the grin on his lips was perfectly clear. A soft, rapid pounding vibrated against Rylan's hand. She looked down—her right palm was still on his chest. His heart was racing, his body heat strong under her touch. Eyes wide, she jerked away, her skin feeling immediately empty at the loss of his heat. Despite his inebriation, his expression was bland.

"No adjusting the seat. No changing the radio station. And no talking." He broke away from her and walked toward the door. Rylan spun to hurry after his long strides. Grabbing her bag from the barstool, she reached in her pocket for cash to pay for the beer she hadn't drunk.

The bartender shook his head. "Consider it a Welcome-to-Hell gift."

Chapter Two

Cole, as it turned out, was about as easy on the ears as he was on the eyes. He didn't say more than necessary on the drive to Paint River and spent the majority of it slumped in the seat with his hat pulled down. He didn't even react when she adjusted the seat to account for her much-shorter legs and changed the static-filled radio station for background music.

Rylan drove slowly in the star-dotted darkness, sure a deer would dart out at any moment, especially after paved road turned into two-lane dirt and led her far from civilization. Rylan was almost afraid for her life. If Cole Haywood turned out to be a murderer, she was screwed, and the sweat on her palms and itch of her neck proved her subconscious was considering it. Not that he'd given any indication that he would harm her. Unless she counted the rank scent of beer rolling off him as potential poison.

He'd been giving her short directions—"Turn here" and "Left at next sign"—but beyond that, nothing. She hadn't attempted to make conversation since he kept drifting off. A sober-up nap was exactly what he needed. That and a long, hot shower to peel the layer of cigar smoke off him. Rylan gave Cole a sidelong glance. Underneath the bar smell were notes of pine and cedar, and some kind of fresh, clean deodorant. In a way, it was sexy and heady…and not helping her concentration one bit.

Rylan rolled the window down to push the scents out and keep her sleep-deprived senses alert. Concentrating on the drive helped push away her nonsensical physical reactions to him earlier. She needed sleep, food, and strong coffee, and in the morning, she'd be much better able to interact with Cole Haywood as she did most people: without emotion and as minimally as possible.

A fork in the road appeared in the headlights. Cole was snoring softly. Rylan flicked his leg, and he jerked. "Left or right?"

He startled just a touch, then gave an annoyed sigh. "Right." His hat was pulled over his face, his long body languid in the seat. "Just keep right. It'll take you to the main gate."

The gate was a huge arch of timber beams supporting a long, rectangular sign that read PAINT RIVER RANCH, EST. 1878. Rylan drove through the gate and down a long, curving drive. Several buildings made hulking shadows on both sides until the main house, a lumbering post-and-beam creation, stretched out before them. A covered deck wrapped around one side, tiny white lights twined around the deck beams. Railroad lanterns glowed softly on the left side of each step going up. A stone chimney and tall, peaked windows framed by chinked logs were the sum of what she could see in the evening light. But even that little bit took her breath away. Maybe this was just what she needed after all.

Rylan parked and slid out of the truck, taking a step back just to take it all in. Expectations or not, this was well beyond anything her brain could have cooked up. This trip now had two things going for it: one sexy as hell, albeit drunk, cowboy, and one beyond-amazing ranch house. Big-ass score.

Cole slid out with a groan, rubbed his belly, wandered to the porch, and disappeared into the house before she could grab her bag from the backseat. Cowboys and chivalry and all that? A fat lie. Rylan lugged her duffel and walked tentatively to the stairs. She paused at the door, feeling that it was too brazen to simply walk in as Cole had. This was his home, and she was just the help—the new help, who had no idea who or where anyone was.

She knocked. Once. Twice. No one came to the door. Antsy now, she knocked again, looking for a doorbell or something that someone might actually hear in the massive house, when the door flew open.

"For Chrissake, just come in!" Cole's shirtless body took up the entire entrance. His muscled torso gleamed in the cast of light and shadow from inside. Dark hair curled over his chest, narrowing down the length of cut-and-sculpted abs. Rylan swallowed hard and looked away. The flutters in her belly were sudden and unwelcome. Half blocking the door, Cole made no further attempt to get out of the way, forcing her to squeeze between his naked chest and the doorframe to get in. She was tempted to quietly jab him in the gut with her elbow as she passed, on principle.

She barely had time to take in her surroundings as he stomped off, making her hurry to keep up. He was remarkably steady considering how unsteady he'd been at the bar. That must have been one hell of a power nap on the ride home.

The entryway spilled into an open floor plan—they passed a dining room, living room, and went down a hallway. A whitewashed plank door sat at the end of the hall. Cole pushed in the door and gave a grand wave of his arm.

"Your bedroom. It has a bathroom, and…whatever. I'll tell Ma you're here in the morning. No more banging. On *anything*." He raised his eyebrows expectantly, like he wasn't sure she understood. Rylan's gaze wandered to the sprawling curls covering his chest. They spread nicely over his pectorals, down the narrow strip of tanned skin along his ribcage, and over his—

Jesus. What the fuckity-fuck was wrong with her? She clenched her eyes. "Got it. No banging."

He turned, showing off a strongly muscled back. A tattoo in gray ink on his right shoulder blade caught her eye. She shifted a little to see. The tattoo spelled out "Birdie" in flowing block text, the tail of the *e* looping to connect to a small sparrow in flight. The ink was almost more masculine-beautiful than his perfect ass hugged by worn Wranglers. A little sigh puffed out between her lips as she wondered who Birdie was.

"'Night," he called before he pulled her door shut.

Rylan let out a hard breath. She was deflated, completely done. Grateful for privacy, she slid the duffel bag off her shoulder and froze. The room was softly lit with an antique brass lantern on the bedside table. The walls were all planks—barn board, she guessed, like the door. But these were bathed in a turquoise patina, not unlike Cole's eyes, with a honey-cream trim and white plank ceiling. The headboard was an old garden gate, resplendent with chipped white paint showing the black metal beneath and huge cast rosettes at the corners. She sat on the quilt-covered bed and ran her hands over the intricate hand-stitching that swirled over the boldly colored wedding-ring pattern. The room was perfect, serene. Quiet and comfortable and so unlike the rigid, suffocating, empty home she'd left behind. Rylan lay back and stared at the ceiling, smiling for the first time in what felt like forever.

• • •

"You better knock on that door and wake her ass up," Cole grumbled as he ran a hand over his face. Good thing his younger brother Tucker had woken him up or he'd have overslept—something he definitely didn't have time for today, or any day for that matter. Alcohol never had been his friend. The pounding in his head, nausea in his gut, and fatigue in his bones were beating him ferociously as a reminder.

Tucker scoffed. "Hell no. You do it. You know how chicks are when you get them up too early."

"She's the help. She's supposed to be up early." It was almost 6:00 a.m., a touch later than he was used to getting up but not too early to get the housekeeper started. The details of last night were a bit fuzzy, but he was pretty sure he hadn't told her what time they'd be starting. He'd barely remembered which guest bedroom to put her in. Never mind the details.

"Why the hell am I getting stuck with this?" Tucker crossed his massive arms and pouted, a move that might have worked when they were eight. All it did now was enrage Cole's foul mood even more.

"Because I have paperwork to do *after* I check fence, because I already made plans with Jaxon to fix a window in the training arena, and because you're pissing me off!"

"I hate waking chicks up." Tucker uncrossed his arms and prepared to knock, a grimace on his freshly shaved face.

"Have you ever stayed long enough to wake a woman in the morning?" Cole narrowed his eyes.

Tucker winked and grinned, knocking Cole in the shoulder with a fist. "You make me sound like a pump and dump."

Cole held back a smile. "That's because you are."

Tucker rolled his eyes. "Not nice, big brother."

Cole smiled despite himself. Since their father's unexpected death last year, they were still working on finding their stride in running the ranch without his strict, carefully planned control. Cole had assumed his father's role as general manager for both the tourist and ranching operations; Tucker took on managing the cattle. And though they were satisfied to be out from under Cooper Haywood's thumb, sometimes it got a little tense and hectic. He and Tucker butted heads over just about everything, yet Cole could always count on Tucker to lighten the mood.

Right now, he only wanted to count on Tucker to take this woman off his hands. "Knock on Rhianna's door."

The door cracked open, startling them both. "It's Rylan, actually. And I've been up since four so no problem there."

Tucker took a step back as the door swung wider and a

long-legged, deliciously full-in-the-hip woman stepped out. Cole did a double take, his scalp exploding in little tingles. Was this the same chick from last night? Her brown hair was piled high in some sort of messy bun. She had no makeup on, her heavily lashed gray eyes bright. And amused.

Cole groaned—she'd heard every word.

Tucker gave Cole a questioning look. "Damn, Cole, you didn't say she was—"

Rylan scratched beside her eye with one finger, observing them both. Cole looked from Rylan to Tucker, recalling how unflinchingly she had stood up to him last night. She'd been one provocation away from turning into a little hellcat, or at least, that's how his soggy brain remembered it. Right now she looked a little uncomfortable.

Her brows arched. "Was what?" Her high, round cheekbones blossomed pink, highlighting the sensual lines of her face.

"How old are you?" Tucker burst out. "I was expecting, you know, someone older. Not…"

Rylan laughed, a soft sound that padded the ache in Cole's head as she shook Tucker's hand. He watched the exchange, trying like hell to remember all of their meeting last night, but it was a blur. Her dark-brown hair had floated around her shoulders, gleaming like mink in the lights. He remembered wanting to touch it—wait, he had touched it, and it was smooth and silky. His fingers itched in response to the memory. Cole balled a fist before he did something stupid like reach out and pet her. He recalled asking her if she was coming on to him, too, and he cursed softly. Drinking to drown emotions was never a good idea, and last night was no exception.

Rylan looked pointedly at him, as if she was remembering things of her own. Cole's face tingled.

"I'm thirty until December," she said. "Then I'll be a little closer to grandma age."

She shifted her weight from one foot to the other, pulling Cole's attention back to the full curve of her hips and the length of her legs. Her jeans looked old and worn, and outlined her body just enough to hint at an hourglass figure that looked as firm as it was curvy. He wished she'd uncross her arms so he could see all of her.

All of Rylan.

The hired help.

What the hell was he doing? He looked away, but not before his libido decided to wake up and do sit-ups against the front of his jeans. She was a pretty, new staff member. No big deal. He'd already been down that road, and that had turned into a costly mistake. Thanks to his mess, the ranch now had a written rule against fraternizing with employees—an addition to the staff handbook he wasn't proud to have spearheaded by his failed example. In an uncouth way, it had become a teasing-but-not-so-much joke. Whenever Tucker got that twinkle in his eye over an attractive new employee, Cole would slap him on the chest and yell, "Handbook!" It usually resulted in getting punched and listening to Tucker bitch, but there had been no other disasters since.

Cole checked his watch. "Tucker is going to show you around."

Rylan nodded, her eyes catching his for just a second before he turned to leave. He brushed off a breathless little feeling that welled at the weight of her gaze. Damned if he'd be falling for that shit again anytime soon.

Chapter Three

One look at the older woman who met them in the kitchen and Rylan knew she was Maeve Haywood. Her turquoise-blue eyes gave it away. She'd passed that gene along to Cole like a champ. Tucker moved aside to make coffee while Maeve wrapped Rylan in a hug.

Rylan went stiff.

"I'm so sorry about the mix-up yesterday. It was good luck that Cole was in town, despite where you two ran into each other." Maeve patted Rylan's back and pulled away with a welcoming smile. Rylan forced off the shock of being enveloped by a complete stranger. She never had been one for blatant affection, especially after having a husband who spent more time with his hands on other women than on her. Maeve's expression of immediate acceptance settled Rylan's nerves a bit, giving her the fleeting sensation of being a long-lost relative instead of the help.

"I was awake when he stumbled in with you last night,"

Maeve continued. "I made him fill me in after you'd gone to bed, drunk as he was."

"Dumbass." Tucker snickered behind them, and then his cell phone rang. He ducked out of the room to answer.

Maeve shook her head and led Rylan to a stool by the breakfast bar. "I hope he wasn't too—"

Rylan waved a hand, not wanting her bad first impression with Cole to taint her first moments with Maeve. She actually cared what Maeve thought of her, considering she'd been hired to assist *her* with running the household. "It was fine, Mrs. Haywood. I'm sorry if we woke you."

Maeve reached for a mug from a neatly stacked row near the large stainless steel coffeemaker. It shook slightly in her hand while she set it in front of Rylan.

"You didn't. I'm used to the boys coming in at all hours. And please, call me Maeve."

Maeve turned to open a drawer, and Rylan grabbed the opportunity to look around. The kitchen was decked out with granite countertops, rich cherry cabinets, stainless steel everything, perfect patina on the worn hardwood floors. The breakfast bar separated the kitchen from the dining room, where an oblong table sat in the middle, large enough to seat twenty or more. Peaked windows rose to the cathedral ceiling above a set of French doors that showed off the mountain range. To the right was a spacious living room, adorned with leather furniture and a floor-to-ceiling river stone fireplace. Dark-brown logs with gray chinking between them created the walls, giving the space a rustic vibe.

Excitement lurched in her chest at the beauty of the place. Until she saw a small pink blanket thrown over the side of an armchair.

Rylan's gut sank, her brain buzzing as she recognized the outline of a princess's face on the side of the blanket. *Oh, God.*

"Ma, what are you doing up so early?" Rylan's stomach completely bottomed out in response to the deep voice. She snapped her gaze away from the blanket as Cole appeared in the kitchen with his hat in one hand. He gave Rylan a fleeting glance, his eyes narrowing a bit before placing a kiss on Maeve's cheek.

"Go back to bed. Tucker is going to show her around." He squeezed Maeve's shoulder affectionately.

She waved him off with a loving smile. "Oh, hush."

Tucker walked back in the room, tucked his cell phone into his back pocket, and picked up the coffeepot, tilting it in Cole's direction. "Thought you had things to do."

Cole took the coffee with a snort. "I was checking to make sure Birdie was still asleep." Rylan thought of the tattoo on Cole's shoulder, her brain riffling through all the possibilities of who Birdie might be. A slow, sinking feeling made her insides heavy—Birdie might be the owner of that blanket, a child. Holding in a blossom of panic, Rylan looked at the counter and tapped her finger over the rim of her mug.

The sounds of coffee being poured and boots shuffling on the floor calmed her, drew her back to her surroundings, though a soft throb had started behind her temple. Children were never mentioned during the interview process. But what if—

Maeve came around the breakfast bar to sit next to her and patted the back of her hand with an affectionate smile. "Did you get enough sleep, Rylan?" A familiar unrest was brewing beneath her ribs, fueling the buzzing in her head and the zing of adrenaline in her veins. Rylan managed to nod and hoped she'd smiled.

"See you later." Tucker flipped a white hat over his red-brown hair.

"Like hell." Cole filled Maeve's cup.

Tucker's devilish grin made Rylan smile despite the lump in her throat. Serious Cole, troublemaker Tucker. And the family dynamics were just beginning. She crossed her ankles and leaned her forearms on the counter, letting the cool granite seep into her skin.

"We've got a broken fence and loose cattle. I'm out of here." He skirted around Cole, wagged his eyebrows at his brother, and left. Cole's stony expression softened a bit as he shook his head. He turned to put the coffeepot away when Maeve cleared her throat.

"Rylan, would you like some coffee?" Maeve looked pointedly at Cole.

Rylan gave a little nod, not really caring if she had coffee or not. A deep restlessness brewed throughout her body, making her want to get up and move, run, anything to stop it from becoming more potent. *Damn, not now.* Though the sudden rush of her flight instinct and anxiety like this was as much a part of her life as breathing, Rylan was still never fully prepared when it came on.

"Y-yes, please." Her mug made a slight grinding sound as she slid it the arm's length across the marble counter. Cole turned and walked over. A deep furrow marked his brow. His eyes were dark, impatient, when they grabbed hers. He placed the pot over her mug and paused for two beats before pouring her a cup, never releasing her gaze. Whatever Cole had been drinking last night caught up with him this morning. He looked exhausted. She had half a mind to ask him who was ornery now, but instead pulled her mug back and sipped the burning liquid to hold her tongue and calm her rampant nerves.

"I'm going to show Rylan around the ranch." Maeve tucked a lock of bobbed ash-blond hair behind her ear. Little crow's feet decorated the outer corners of her eyes. Despite those little marks of age and the subtle creases around her mouth, time looked like it had forgotten about her.

Cole's voice was gravelly. "You can't walk the grounds yourself right now, Ma. You might fal—"

"Fine, then come along and give me your arm," Maeve interrupted. She turned to Rylan. "I love the ranch this early in the morning. You'll see why." She rose unsteadily, bracing herself on the counter with one hand. Cole was at Maeve's side instantly, grabbing her elbow to steady her. Maeve shook her head as they exchanged words Rylan couldn't hear.

As a cop, she'd been trained to watch the subtleties of body language and expression for clues to a person's true nature. Cole's entire demeanor changed, impatience melting into concern, the hard lines around his eyes softening. A small smile pulled at Rylan's lips as warmth flooded her veins. Boys were supposed to love their mamas, and Cole seemed to fit that bill just fine.

Maeve tossed Rylan a reassuring glance. "Ready?" They walked to the French doors and out onto the wraparound deck. The new light of day was softly gold and peach, the early June air cool with a hint of the warmth to come. Rylan paused in awe. The mountain range in the distance was breathtaking. Peaks disappeared into pristine white clouds, stone reflecting blue and black and gray in the light. Zen didn't cut it. It was hurt-deep-in-your-chest beautiful. In just that one moment, it was easy to forget about the family she no longer had and the legal trouble still hanging over her head. Not much could do that these days. Rylan breathed it in.

A gruff voice pulled her away. "You coming?" Cole eyed her over his shoulder as he settled Maeve's hand in the bend of his arm. Man, he was good at being edgy. She looked at the mountains as she went down the steps, grasping for that surreal feeling again, but it was gone. She hoped not for good, though, because it was exactly what she needed.

As they walked, Maeve explained that Paint River was a ranch hybrid. In addition to accommodating tourist and recreation activities like fishing, hiking, and guided horseback rides, as well as providing facilities for weddings and retreats, Paint River was a 38,000-acre working ranch. It housed 650 head of Black Angus cattle, along with the registered quarter horse stock that Cole and Tucker managed for breeding, ranch work, and the show ring. Rylan had grown up on a dairy farm, but a spread of this magnitude was hard to wrap her head around.

They walked a dirt road to the right of the ranch house, passing a two-story log building that served as an office and small store for guests and moving toward a row of bright-red cottages trimmed in white, reminding Rylan of the old Wisconsin barns back home. Fifteen cottages stood in a tidy row, hanging plants and a rocking chair on each small front porch. Behind the cottages was wide-open flatland dotted with wildflowers, the distant mountain range embracing the property. Hiking trails cut through the grass, lined with blue-tipped markers. Perfect for a run.

Taking the same driveway back the way they'd come, they continued past the ranch house and down a slight hill. The scene below was a rustic contrast from the manicured beauty of the guest side of the property. Three lumbering barns—one painted brown, one green, and one weathered gray barn board—sat side by side. A bunkhouse crafted from yellowish pine logs with brown chinking housed fifteen ranch hands who lived on site. Smaller buildings were scattered here and there, large pens with metal fencing dotting the landscape.

This part of the ranch was teeming with activity. Cowboys on horses rode past with dogs following along; a truck and trailer rambled down the drive. Two large pens were filled with cattle, another with a handful of horses munching on hay.

"Want to tour the barns?" Maeve asked.

The barn back home had been her personal sanctuary as a kid. The perfect place to get lost in thought or heal a broken heart. Rylan missed the bustle of activity and hard work that accompanied this kind of life. She'd missed milking the cows with her father at the crack of dawn every morning, cutting hay in the fields, and the freedom that could be found on the back of a horse. She'd given that all up for life as a city cop married to a man who'd rather she forget she was ever a poor farmer's daughter. Immersing herself in ranch life had been too promising to resist when she'd applied for the job here.

"I'd love to!" Rylan said.

A shadow of a smile crossed Cole's lips at her eager statement. He tipped his chin, the brim of his hat partially covering his face. It didn't hide the way he glanced at her feet and worked his way up. Rylan's cheeks went hot by the time he got to her chest.

"Ma, I'm burning daylight. Can we do this another time? It's not like she's going anywhere."

She? *I have a name, ass-hat.*

Rylan cocked her head to the side. Despite the way he seemed to dismiss her, the tingle in the very bottom of her belly made it hard to deny how good he looked. Sexy. Irritating. Intriguing. *Employer.* The part of her brain that found him deliciously attractive grumbled while the half that considered him off-limits hoped she wouldn't have to interact too much more with Cole. Work—and healing—might be too darn difficult with him around.

Smiling sweetly while she threw curse words at him in her mind, Rylan gave an agreeable nod. "That's fine. I'll walk Maeve back." Rylan held her arm to Maeve's free hand. Cole stared her down. She stared back, her heart hitching painfully fast. The battered brown hat sat just so on his head, a lick of black curls peeking out around his ears. He hadn't shaved last night's stubble—it was darker, thicker. Sexier.

Just when Rylan thought her retinas would combust from the intensity of his gaze, Cole tipped his hat to his mother and walked toward the barns.

Maeve chuckled as they turned back toward the house. "You won't see much of Cole. He oversees everything that happens on the ranch. To say he's busy is an understatement." Rylan should have felt reassured by that, but disappointment crept in.

Maeve tripped a little on the uneven ground, her body trembling slightly as if she were cold. Rylan almost asked if she was ill but clamped her lips together before the words escaped. Whatever was going on with Maeve's health, she apparently wasn't volunteering information.

Back in the ranch house, Maeve gave Rylan a walk-through. The house was resplendent in wood and stone, with rustic touches that echoed the Western landscape. They passed the stairway, paused at the bottom but didn't go up.

"I sleep in the alcove bedroom behind the kitchen," Maeve said. "Everyone else is upstairs. So we'll all just leave laundry outside our doors for you to pick up each day, if that works."

Rylan followed along behind Maeve's still-shaky steps as they went to the laundry room and talked household duties. Back in the kitchen, Maeve showed Rylan a weekly meal plan and where the cooking necessities were located.

"I'll leave most of the cooking up to you. Don't worry about breakfast—that's just strong coffee around here. Boys'll come up around noon, sometimes, for a sandwich. Otherwise, they'll be in when they can for dinner. I usually get it ready and keep it in the oven to stay warm."

"Reminds me of my dad and brother back home. I'd cook one big meal a day. Sometimes they'd run in like the devil was after them and shovel it down so fast, they wouldn't even speak. During harvest, I'd be lucky to see them at all," Rylan said, the wistfulness in her voice sending rockets through her chest. The memory was fast and sudden. So were the longing and bittersweet joy that went with it. Why the hell that had just come out of her mouth, she had no idea. Talking about herself wasn't high on her list of things necessary for getting through life.

Maeve sat while Rylan refilled their coffee cups and

started another pot.

"Seems strange to people who don't ranch for a living—grown men living with their mother. But we all need each other to make this place work." Maeve's face took on a forlorn look as she rimmed the handle of her cup with a finger. "I have another son, Levi. He's a Marine, currently in Afghanistan, and my husband passed last year. Cole and Tucker work hard—real hard—to keep this place going and fill in the gaps."

Rylan stirred sugar into her coffee. She and her brother had stayed on the farm until wanderlust took hold of them both. She'd gone to the police academy, her brother to work abroad as a photographer. Shortly after, their father sold out. All these years later, Rylan still felt a little guilty for not staying closer to her father to help.

Rylan didn't question that Cole busted his ass. Everything about him screamed dedication, including the scowl that probably meant he always had too much on his mind. She'd always loved hardworking country boys. How she'd ended up married to a judge who freaked at the first sign of dirt under his fingernails was still a mystery.

A shaggy gray-and-brown dog burst into the room, stopping at Maeve's feet and bumping her legs with his head. The sound of little feet followed right behind.

"Doggie!" a small voice cried out. A tiny little girl, maybe four years old, followed the dog and clambered onto Maeve's lap. Maeve welcomed her with a kiss and snuggle. Rylan's chest turned to stone, weighing her down, squeezing out her breath.

"Good morning!" Maeve gave her another kiss. The child studied Rylan with huge, emerald-green eyes—turquoise in the light—and popped a finger in her rosebud mouth.

"This little sprite is Bernadette, Birdie as we call her. Cole's daughter. She's an early riser, just like her daddy. Birdie, can you say hello to Miss Rylan? She's the new housekeeper."

The child might have said something, but Rylan didn't know. Her ears were ringing with a rush of emotion so strong, she almost tipped backward off the stool. The counter was cool as she managed to grip it to steady herself.

Cole's daughter? She thought fleetingly of his tattoo. The little girl was beautiful, but no one had said anything about a kid.

"Rylan, are you all right?" Maeve eyed her steadily, and Rylan nodded, realizing how crazy she had probably looked just then. But shit... If she'd known there were children in the house, would she have still come? Birdie nibbled a tiny thumb, the ruffles of her pink Dora the Explorer nightgown hiding her feet, save two little toes that peeked out.

A little girl in pink ruffles—maybe how her Rachel would have looked now.

"Yes," she responded a little too quickly. *No!* "Nice... to meet you, Birdie." That was the best she could manage, even with Maeve's suspicious smile. Maybe it was concern— Rylan didn't know, didn't care. She needed to get out of the room before she threw up all over the beautiful kitchen.

"Will you excuse me?" Rylan dashed off the stool without waiting for an answer and hurried to her room. She sank behind the closed door, hugging her knees and stifling the sobs that raged like an angry mob in her throat. Suddenly, being locked away in her house again seemed like a great idea. There weren't any children there. Not anymore.

Chapter Four

The new day was alive with color as red and yellow rays of sun cascaded over the mountain range. The sky was clear, promising warmth and good weather. Cole checked to make sure Birdie was still sleeping and found her snoring softly, snuggled in her blanket. Some days she seemed to be outgrowing her tendency to wake at four or five in the morning, though he could never count on when she might decide to sleep in or not. He was always glad to find her out cold when he left in the morning so he could get a few things done before she woke. Not that he'd complain if she was up early. He'd keep Birdie on his horse with him all day if he could. It just wasn't safe for a four-year-old to tag along all the time.

Maeve's health made it harder for her to care for Birdie than before, too, and the guilt Cole experienced when he watched his mother struggle to keep up with the child was crushing. Maeve insisted she was fine, but deep down, Cole knew it was time to look for a nanny. Though it hadn't been in the job description, he'd hoped whoever they hired as a housekeeper could double with child care duty here and there.

Rylan had a clean background check and record of decorated service as a police officer. He'd checked up on her a little when Maeve said she was going to hire her. *Trying to simplify my life,* she'd put on her application. She seemed like the perfect candidate to approach about lending a hand—until Maeve filled him in on how Rylan had freaked out at meeting Birdie the day before. Maybe she wasn't as good a fit as he'd thought.

Cole slid a hand through his hair, trying to forget how he'd lain awake much of the night thinking about Rylan. Pondering the housekeeper—her long legs and the way her hair wisped around her face, how her eyes changed from silver to pewter when her feathers got ruffled, what brought her to Paint River—would lead to nothing but trouble. But damn if his blood hadn't gotten a little hot, tempting him to think a little more. He'd had to clamp down on his wayward brain hard and fast. Getting romantically involved with an employee was something he'd never, ever do again.

Growing up with a cold, anger-fueled father left a gap Cole had always hoped to fill with a family of his own. Love and lots of it. A peaceful, welcoming home.

Tried. Failed.

His marriage had been a sham, but it had given him Birdie, and she was enough. She was his, and he loved her more than he'd ever be able to express. But for a flickering moment yesterday, his mind had constructed a nice little image of Rylan holding Birdie on her hip, and it had hit him hard—maybe his mind was putting together a visual for what his soul wanted deep down. Telling him that it was okay to want more.

Squash. He'd made dirt out of that little nugget right quick.

He went to the kitchen and filled his coffee mug, glad to see a fresh pot had been brewed, and pushed back thoughts of Rylan only to find her sitting sideways on the deck steps. He was flooded again with things he was better off not thinking about. Five in the morning and she was holding a steaming mug, her hair glossy as it fell to the middle of her back, the rich brown hues offset by the cream-colored sweater she wore, twisting his gut up in knots. Her eyes were closed, a small smile on pink, slightly parted, beautiful lips. She was enjoying the morning, the moment, and damn if he wasn't tempted to sit down and enjoy it with her.

He mentally punched himself as he stepped out the doors and onto the deck. An uncertain smudge touched her lips when her eyes flew open and she saw him. The urge to sit down next to her and enjoy the sunrise just plain pissed him off. Cole frowned. He couldn't have this…this reaction to her.

"Shouldn't you be working?" He flipped his hat on and crossed to the stairs, glancing at her quickly before diverting his gaze so he didn't get lost in the way her hair shone in the sunlight or the sleepy flush on her cheeks.

"Maeve said my working hours are 6:00 a.m. to 6:00 p.m. It's only five fifteen, which means I can sip my coffee for another forty-five goddamn minutes if I want." The lilt in her voice made him pause on the last step. Was she teasing him? Challenging him? Being sarcastic? Even as he tried to determine her mood—and wonder why he cared—his mind wandered to her abbreviated tour yesterday.

His brain started to rattle in protest to his thoughts.

Don't do it, don't do it, don't do—

"Then I suppose you have time to tour the barns, huh?" he asked as he descended the steps.

Shit. Then he pulled himself together. After the way he'd acted when they met, he owed her a little hospitality to smooth things over. That's all.

The sound of a mug being set on the wooden steps broke the small silence. "I shouldn't." Her voice was soft, as if she was trying to talk herself out of it.

Disappointment flittered through him. He gave a curt nod, cursed himself for offering in the first place, and started to walk away when the sound of her scrambling off the steps and hurrying down the gravel made the back of his neck tingle. Then she was next to him, close enough that he could touch her if he wanted to but far enough away to give them a buffer.

Their footfalls found an immediate rhythm. She put her hands in her back pockets, her eyes wide and eager as she took in her surroundings. Cole slowed his pace, though this was really the last thing he had time to be doing. Little flickers crossed her face as she looked around, but she didn't speak. Most women talked his damn ear off, and as much as that drove him nuts, he liked the sound of Rylan's voice and wished she'd say something to let him hear it.

"So you ride?" Cole asked as they approached the slight hill that led to the barns. She glanced at him and nodded. *Damn. Thwarted.* "Western saddle, I hope?"

Her head turned his way again, but her eyes didn't meet his for nearly long enough. The quick flash of silver in her gaze left him longing for more. Rylan rotated her shoulders just a bit, her breasts pushing against her shirt. He recalled the slope and rise of the curves she had under that boxy sweater. The heat in his groin remembered too.

"Yeah, but truthfully, I prefer bareback."

The sudden image he had of Rylan riding bareback didn't have a thing to do with a horse. Cole adjusted his hat to give his hands something to do and picked up his pace. This simple, early-morning walk was nice, but considering he was the glue that held a multimillion-dollar ranch and tourist operation together, a morning stroll did nothing to erase his to-do list. Besides, the more he ambled, the more his mind took him and his cock places they shouldn't be going.

The stable was busy when they entered, ranch hands getting ready for the day. Cole made brief introductions as they walked the rubber-padded aisle between two rows of stalls. The fruity scent of her freshly washed hair mixed in with the smell of hay and leather and horse, and in an enticing way, it fit just right. That eagerness was on her face again, her cheeks flushed and eyes bright with excitement. Most of the horses were out to pasture, but he'd kept in a few, including the new black-and-white stallion he'd bought the previous week.

Angry banging on the last stall on the left told Cole that Pana Bar Noir still didn't like his new home very much. Another bang followed by a sharp squeal had Cole taking long strides down the aisle to Pana's stall. Rylan popped up next to him, a long, appreciative sigh rolling out of her. Pana's mostly black coat was broken up with curving white patches along his huge hips and under his belly. His right leg was white and so was most of his face, though both eyes were surrounded in black like a mask. It made the stunning, liquid blue of the stallion's eyes shine.

"He's gorgeous!" The words tumbled out fast. Her cheeks blushed darker, as if the admission embarrassed her. Pana shook his head violently, strands of his long black mane coming through the bars on the top half of the stall door. Rylan gripped the bars, her eyes wide.

"He's a goddamn pain in the ass. Aren't you, Pana?" Cole dug around in his pocket. The stallion stopped his fidgeting, his left ear cocking to the side. Rylan reached three fingers between the bars. Pana bumped her hand with his nose, and realizing she didn't have what he wanted, turned to Cole. Cole nudged Rylan's arm with his elbow, and when she withdrew her hand from between the bars, he tipped sugar into her palm.

"He's kind of addicted to the stuff. I bring him some every morning."

She chuckled and stroked the horse's nose with her other hand as he lipped the sugar from her palm. "He's a beautiful paint."

Warmth filled Cole's chest at the compliment. When the sugar was gone, Cole led Rylan across the aisle and unlocked a stall door, letting it swing open. A bulky quarter horse with a color pattern similar to Pana's wandered out and stopped like an obedient puppy at Cole's side.

"This is Sisko. Just as pretty as Pana but not nearly as crazy."

Rylan's hands were on the horse in a flash. Cole couldn't help but follow the path of her fingers with his eyes as she stroked Sisko's black-and-white patched face. Her hands were narrow, fingers long and topped with neatly trimmed nails. No gaudy, bright-pink nail polish or fake nails and certainly no rings—not even a line to show where a wedding ring may have been. That little detail made him happier than it should have.

Rylan's hands followed Sisko's back, palms rounding over his bulky hips, almost as if she was sculpting him with her touch. She was appraising him with her hands and her eyes, and Cole felt a flicker of admiration. She knew her way around a horse. If her hands were any indication, she probably knew her way around a man, too. A quick shot of lightning zapped him in the groin. Cole closed his eyes for a second, realizing it had been way too long since he'd taken time off. His body was reacting to Rylan as a red flag that it was time for a break and to find himself some female company—away from the ranch.

She traced the dark outline of the Paint River Ranch brand on Sisko's hip. The *P* and upside-down, backward *R* surrounded by a circle had been placed in a white patch, but the hair had grown in black, making the brand pop.

"Born here?" she asked, turning to look at him.

"Yeah. We breed for color patterns that stand out in the show ring." He was proud of the breeding program he and Tucker started six years ago. Their paint stock threw some of the best-colored quarter horses anywhere. Paint River had a two-year waiting list for foal sales, and their mature, started-under-saddle stock commanded some of the highest prices in the state.

She gave an appreciative nod that revved his ego and his libido in one swoop. Cole leaned one elbow against the stall. Sunlight streamed in, casting rusty, barn-red highlights in her deep brown hair. The sounds of horses crunching hay, men talking, and tack being rustled around came together and danced in his head, but the sound that broke free was

Rylan's soft voice, talking to Sisko in quiet, hushed tones. A couple minutes passed, maybe even ten. He didn't know because that sound was carrying him away.

Cole's phone buzzed, making him jerk. He grabbed it to see a text message pop up.

Cole, we need to talk. Call me.

The ease that had settled inside him was ripped away, frustration and a heavy dose of anger replacing it. His ex-wife didn't like being ignored, hadn't gotten the hint when he didn't return any of her voice messages or texts in the past week. When she wanted to meet and talk after a nearly four-year absence, he was pretty sure her idea of conversation topics involved one of two things: money or Birdie. With his luck, probably both. Livy popping up out of the blue had driven him to the rare drinking binge he'd been on when he'd met Rylan.

Rylan. Who was a Paint River employee, just as Livy had been when he'd fallen for her. He jammed the phone into his back pocket. He didn't have any business feeling at ease around Rylan. The text message just reminded him why.

He cleared his throat impatiently. "If you're done making love to him, I need to get to work. And so do you."

Rylan's head snapped up, the pleasure slipping from her face. She let her hands fall away from Sisko and stepped back. He was being an ass, but Cole couldn't allow himself to care about hurting her feelings. The more he kept her at arm's length, the better.

"Yes, sir." Her reply was quiet but firm, with a slight edge of snark. She pushed up her sleeves as Cole whistled for Sisko to get back in the stall. A tendril of guilt uncurled and slapped him. He really disliked seeing the excitement gone from her face.

"You can consider Sisko yours to use while you're here," Cole offered neutrally as he latched the stall door and turned back into the aisle. "He's bombproof." He nodded for her to follow, taking her to the very back of the stable and opening a set of large double doors that led to the enclosed riding arena.

"If it's raining or snowing, you're free to ride in here."

"Impressive," she said softly.

Cole replied curtly, "We hold cutting horse trials here each spring. In fact, you just missed it. We also have a community festival here in the late summer. Some area horse trainers come in each week, too. There's a schedule here." He pointed to a paper taped to the door. "If it's free, and you're done with your work, go ahead and use it."

Cole shut the doors and headed back the way they'd come, needing space from her damn fruity-smelling hair. She didn't say anything as they walked to the exit.

"You know your way to the house." He dismissed her, waving toward the door. The irritation inside him was prickly and demanding. Rylan didn't respond, just walked past him. The sleeve of her sweater brushed against his bare forearm, sending shocks of pleasure over his skin at the same time the regret sank like a rock in his gut. He wiped the sensation off with a quick glide of his palm, but the quiver deep inside didn't go away.

Cole gave Rylan's retreating form one last glance before turning and storming into the stable office. Leave it to his ex-wife to pop up and remind him why he couldn't trust a woman again, why he was better off alone.

Chapter Five

Birdie was determined to keep Rylan company. While she studied the binder of responsibilities and expectations for her role at the kitchen counter, the little girl sat on the floor and colored. When she walked through the house, memorizing the layout, Birdie tagged a short distance behind. Being in the constant sight of a four-year-old was unnerving. Rylan was struggling with the fact that there was a child under the same roof, a child she'd come into contact with every single day, and it was harder to try to acclimate to that when said child wouldn't leave her alone.

Part of the reason she'd left Wisconsin was to try to re-structure the memories of her daughter. She'd hoped that by getting away from the place where Rachel had been born and lived, her memories would lose some of their bitter edge and turn sweeter. Maybe she'd even finally come to terms with her guilt over how Rachel died.

Only her second day at Paint River and she was

immersed in crayons, dolls on the living room floor, and a little sprite playing cat and mouse with her emotions. Only eighteen months old when she'd died, Rachel would have looked a lot like Birdie did now, Rylan imagined. Blond curls, round cheeks, perfect little lips—she would have probably followed at her heels, everywhere, too. Damn, this wasn't fair. How could she reconcile with her past when a ghost was staring at her?

Just when Rylan thought she couldn't handle the ache in her chest any longer, Maeve wrangled Birdie down for a nap, and then pulled Rylan in for sweet tea and a break. Rylan didn't touch her tea, could barely make eye contact with Maeve as she struggled with memories of Rachel that left her arms aching and empty.

"I'm sorry if she got underfoot," Maeve said around sips of tea. "Cole and Birdie's mother divorced when Birdie was an infant. She's never known her mother, and my sister, Penny, and I are the only women in her life. She's just curious about you."

The mention of Cole threw her further into a tangled web of restlessness. She'd loved the smile on his face yesterday in the barn, how he watched her as she'd gotten to know Sisko. Most of all, she'd loved his company—how at ease she'd felt. Considering how they'd met, "relaxed" wasn't a term she associated with Cole Haywood. She guessed she shouldn't have been surprised when he'd gone back to impatient and unfriendly, giving her a good reminder that she'd come here to work, and heal, and figure out what to do with her life next. She needed to focus, not worry about how Cole or anyone else regarded her beyond her role as their housekeeper.

She spent the rest of the day finding her stride as she went through her chore list, pleased with the sense of satisfaction she'd experienced over having something to do. All that time hiding in her house, pacing and sitting idle and flipping through television channels, completely erased her sense of purpose, while very nearly erasing her sense of self. She'd gone from a full-time police officer to a full-time mother to a woman with nothing except time on her hands.

As she helped Maeve get supper on the table that night—pot roast, green beans, coleslaw, fresh bread, and molasses cookies—Rylan felt as if she'd completed something important. For the first time in way too long, she'd had a remarkably productive day.

Birdie was sitting at the kitchen table and shrieked when Cole walked in. She slipped off the chair so fast to run into his arms, she nearly fell face-first. "Daddy!"

Cole scooped Birdie up and spun her in a circle, smiling as she giggled and nuzzled into his neck.

"Did you wash your hands, little girl?" He made a great show of flipping her hands over and inspecting each finger. Cole frowned and held up his own hands. Birdie made a disgusted face.

"You wash your hands, Daddy. Come on." Birdie tugged his sleeve, pulling him to the hallway bathroom. Tucker came in next, looking no less dirty than Cole. He went to the kitchen sink, filled one side with water and dunked his face right in. Rylan snickered a little, recalling how her father and brother would come into the house grubby from milking cows and cleaning the barn. Her brother would hose his face with the kitchen sink sprayer when the summer heat made the grime stick hard to his skin. Nostalgia tiptoed in and left dirty footprints on Rylan's satisfaction.

Maeve gave a pleased smile, then turned it on Rylan. "It's about time we all get to eat together. I told them to be in for supper, or else."

Last night, Rylan, Maeve, and Birdie had eaten at the breakfast bar together, leaving plates for the men in the oven. Tonight, the table looked fit for a holiday feast. Rylan helped Maeve finish setting out the food as Cole and Birdie came back in. Cole's hair was wet, his bangs slicked back over his head like he'd been running his fingers through it, the ends curling every which way. He glanced her way as Birdie propped herself up on his knee. He bounced her. She giggled. Rylan's heart swelled and threatened to burst right in half.

Cole poked Birdie's nose. "Love you, baby girl."

Rip.

Rylan skirted back to the kitchen and did busywork, trying to ease out the twist beneath her ribs. Seeing them all together—especially Birdie wrapped so sweetly in her father's love—had tears clawing at the backs of her eyes. It was a blatant reminder that she was alone. That she had nothing.

"Rylan, come sit if you'd like," Maeve called warmly. Chairs moved, dishes clinked, voices connected. Rylan froze, braced herself with one arm on the far counter, wishing a gaping cavity would open in the floor and suck her right the hell outta there.

"Rylan?" Maeve's chair scooted across the hardwood floor. Rylan's pulse pumped.

"Oh, no, thank you." She edged out of the kitchen into the back part of the house and to the laundry room. In the solitude, Rylan organized a shelf of cleaners, folded a load of towels, and paced the perimeter of the space, but the anxiety inside didn't die. This restlessness was an all-consuming constant since Rachel's death. There wasn't anything she could do when the little sphere of unrest bounced around inside her except let it wear itself out.

When she crept back to the kitchen an hour later, everyone was gone. Guilt sliced through her when she saw the table cleared and the dishes neatly stacked. Maeve hadn't said but Rylan considered cleaning up after meals her responsibility, even though it was past her 6:00 p.m. end-of-day. She loaded the plates and glasses that were left into the dishwasher and tidied up. Each time she glanced at the table, she saw Birdie on Cole's knee, and the panic would rise with renewed force.

It was getting dark outside, but screw it. She needed a run.

Rylan changed into shorts and running shoes. There was just enough daylight for her to run the unease away. She'd run until she dropped or the craze within subsided. A quick stretch and she sneaked out the back door before anyone spotted her. Guests and ranch hands were milling about as Rylan walked away from the house, past the cabins to a trail marked with a blue hiking sign. She started at a jog, pleased to see the open-prairie trail was marked every few feet with the blue-tipped posts.

Then she ran. Hard and fast—harder than she had in weeks. She ran as a habit of police training. She ran to forget. Running soothed her like nothing else by forcing every single thought from her head except the tasks at hand: placing one foot in front of the other and breathing. In and out, in and out, steady and calm. When she finally stopped, dusk had claimed the mountain and the flat expanse ahead. Rylan doubled over, hands to her knees. *Damn, that felt good.* It was stupid to go this far with dark falling, but she didn't care—her body was alive with adrenaline, and the bubble inside was momentarily quelled. She was going to revel in it. She rested a bit and eventually started walking back to the house as dusk thickened.

And then the dark came, fast and complete, and her belly quivered with the first full realization that she was alone. In the middle of an open plain. Just as her brain conjured images of ravenous grizzly bears and prowling mountain lions, the vibration of pounding feet up ahead made her pulse thrum so hard it hurt the side of her neck.

"Rylan! Shit, woman!" She recognized Cole's voice a second before a flashlight beam hit her square in the eyes. He cussed. She swore from the pain eating her eyeballs.

"What the hell got into you, coming out here like this? You're lucky one of the men told me you went this way."

Rylan rubbed her eyes, trying to clear the dots. "I've known you literally two days, and I hate you a little more each minute," she hissed.

Cole leaned down in the saddle and grabbed her arm. "Get on the horse!" Alarm jumped her, followed by an excited little tickle between her legs. Aghast, Rylan smacked his hand. A dark henley stretched across his torso, showing off the heavy rise and fall of his chest.

"Don't manhandle me!" She pulled back, her sweat-slick arm sliding free from Cole's grip.

The squeak of leather filled the air as he dismounted his horse and grabbed at her again. He made a disgusted sound and let go, wiping his hand on his thigh. "I said, get on."

His high-handedness inflamed her stubborn side. Rylan ignored him, taking huge strides to get in front of him, the excitement racing through her body getting stronger. If she got on the horse with him, her thighs would be wrapped around Cole's, her chest pressed into the firm heat of his back… She shook her head, thrust up a palm to put space between him and her thoughts. No. *Hell*, no.

"You could have gotten turned around. Worse, wolves like to come this way at night. Now mount the hell up so we can get back." The base of her neck prickled at the mention of wolves, but she steeled herself and kept on walking in the beam of light Cole threw down the trail. She imagined her breasts tight against his back, his rigid abdomen warming her palms. Rylan made fists in response to the thought.

"I'll walk."

He pulled the back of her T-shirt this time. Furious, and more than a little flushed by the feel of his grip on her, Rylan spun to face him, her shirt popping free from his clutch.

"You're infuriating!" Cole snapped.

"Yes, *you* are!" Rylan shot back.

Cole took a step that nearly obliterated the space between them. His body heat radiated to her, his scent of sage and summer air heady and making her veins flush hot. The beam of light reflected off the ground, casting a soft glow over his face—just enough that Rylan could see his anger fade into something else, something that made her thighs clench and her lips tremble and ache. Her chest clamped with the inability to breathe. Just when she thought she might lean forward and fall into him, Cole stepped back.

"We need to get back."

She swallowed hard and nodded, her mouth too dry to form words. The light led the way as she fell into step beside Cole, his horse walking behind him. The ground was a little uneven, causing Rylan to misstep and bump into him. She moved a little farther away but not before she'd felt the goose bumps that rose on his skin when her bare arm had touched his.

"So, what's with missing out on a perfectly good dinner?" Cole's voice was like warm whiskey, slow and luxurious on the intake and pure heat going down. Being beside him, wrapped in his voice, made the last licks of fear over the dark fade away.

"I don't do family time." It might have been the horse, but she was pretty sure Cole grunted at her.

"Family time? It was just dinner."

"Yeah, with your *family* there. I prefer…to be alone." And away from any reminder of the family she'd lost.

"We just happened to be related and starving. Pure coincidence." The lilt in his voice tripped her up inside. She was running full speed ahead on irritation and he threw a little lightheartedness in throw her off. She glanced at him, his profile strong even highlighted in shadow. His mouth hinted at a smile, and the promise was just as sexy as if he'd really let that grin loose. Maybe…if the circumstances were different—if he weren't her boss and she weren't so broken inside—getting to know Cole Haywood better might be something she'd pursue.

Light from the property peeked through the darkness, filling her with disappointment that their walk in the dark was almost over. She scrunched her forehead, knowing she had no business feeling that way. Her inner thigh muscles trembled from the hard run, her body ready to sink into bed and sleep off the exhaustion-dump her fading adrenaline had left behind. Cole looked at her and took a breath like he was going to speak.

Her right foot caught on a stone, and she twisted halfway to the ground. Cole leaned to grab her, one hand going to her lower back, the other to her belly as he righted her. Shivers bred like bunnies all over her body. She froze at the sudden pleasure of being trapped between his hands. She blinked hard—he was standing perfectly still, too. And then his fingers splayed across her abdomen, bunching the T-shirt and making her muscles clench. His other hand shifted to the curve of her lower back, the flashlight he still gripped banging against her bottom.

He was close enough that she could see the flash of desire in his eyes.

"If I didn't know better, I'd think you were trying to get yourself into my arms, Rylan." His husky words punched the breath right out of her.

She shouldn't be, but maybe... *Don't go there!* Rylan smacked his hand away from her middle, and smoothed her shirt when he abruptly let go.

Her voice shook way more than she was happy about. "Your ego would like that too much, *Mr.* Haywood."

He stepped back immediately, the reminder of her role having the effect she'd intended. Clicking to the horse, he walked ahead. Rylan purposely stayed two steps behind to give herself space. Her left arm ached where she'd bumped into him, her belly cold from the loss of his palm against it. When they reached the edge of the property, Cole turned to her.

"Next time, consider running in the daylight."

"Thanks for the tip." Rylan shouldered ahead but paused with a flicker of guilt. She had been stupid to go that far so close to dusk. And he had come to get her out of it.

"Thanks for helping me out," she said, relenting. He stared at her long and hard before heading off to the stable without another word. Rylan looked after him a moment and took a calming breath, realizing the restlessness she'd been fighting all day was gone.

Chapter Six

Cole didn't bother buttoning his shirt as he left his room. Two days had passed since he'd found Rylan on the trail. He'd purposely kept his distance since then, knowing it was better to quench the stirrings of attraction he felt for her now, rather than risk letting it grow. But now he needed her help, and he couldn't avoid her any longer.

He'd turned his cell phone on at 5:00 a.m. and a vicious mix of text messages and appointment reminders screamed that he was already moving too slowly. Hosting a celebrity wedding on the ranch in two days meant they were on the countdown, where stress and chaos—and potential disaster—would ensue, as it always did whenever they hosted an event like this.

Despite the money such high-profile events brought in, Cole hated the stress that went with it. Paint River was supposed to be fully staffed right now to help with preparations, but text messages from three employees not coming in today foiled that plan. And left Rylan to fill some gaps.

He finger-combed his wet hair to keep his too-long bangs out of his eyes and knocked lightly on Rylan's door. Anxiety trickled through him as he waited. She'd blatantly put him in his place with the *Mr. Haywood* barb the last time they'd spoken, and rightly so.

Memo. Noted.

From now on, he'd be professional and brief, and try to stay the hell out of her way as much as possible. Shouldn't be too hard to do on 38,000 acres. The door cracked, revealing the soft outline of Rylan's tall, curvy body, and Cole's mouth went completely dry. The attraction, apparently, hadn't read the employee handbook.

"Morning," she greeted, softly. A warm smile graced her lips. Her hair was damp and pulled over one shoulder. A navy blue V-neck T-shirt hugged her breasts just right, the hem falling just above the waist of her old, worn jeans. His eyes fell to her feet, the glossy red of her toenails making his insides sizzle.

His brain seemed a little heavy all of a sudden. "I…need you."

Her eyebrows arched, pink flushing her cheeks. Cole rubbed the back of his neck with one hand and hurried on. "I need your help. Come with me?" *Smooth, Haywood. Really.*

Her eyes swept his chest. He glanced down—he'd forgotten he still hadn't buttoned his shirt.

"Okay." She left the door open while she slipped on her sandals, and he quickly buttoned up. They walked through the house and outside in silence, the scent of her sweet shampoo a constant attack on his senses. As they descended the deck steps, he slipped a set of keys into her hand. She looked at him questioningly.

He pointed to a white Ford truck parked next to his Chevy. "Keep the keys. That truck is yours to use while you're here."

"Really?" Her eyes lit up. Cole walked between the trucks and leaned an elbow on the side of his pickup's bed. "Have you been up to the tents yet?"

She closed her hand around the keys. "No. Maeve mentioned them, but I haven't had a chance to see them yet."

Cole nodded to some boxes in the back of his truck. "That country singer's wedding is in a couple days. It takes some time to get all those luxury tents ready. Gotta keep the celebrities happy." He reached inside his truck and produced a clipboard, then handed it to her. It had a diagram of a tent, complete with the arrangement of the furniture and a list of things each tent should have inside.

"We have a girl who comes to stage the tents, but she can't come in today, so I'm going to need you to take care of it. Follow me up there." The *tap, tap, tap* of his libido faded away as work mode set in. Cole was suddenly very happy to have too much to do.

"Staging? Isn't that where you put things together to make a room look nice?"

He shrugged. "Yeah." He rounded his truck to the driver's-side door. Rylan was still standing there with the clipboard.

"I'm, uh, not very good at making things look pretty."

"Did you look in the mirror this morning? I'd say you do just fine." The wide-eyed look Rylan whipped at him told Cole he'd said that out loud. Christ. Not daring to look at her again for fear of what might spill out his mouth next, he slid into his truck.

"Let's go," he called through the open passenger window. Cole punched himself into work mode by reciting his mental to-do list as they drove past the cabins. A well-groomed road led through a spread of wild prairie dotted with pink and purple flowers before curving to the right and taking them to a double-panel gate. Cole jumped out and opened it, letting Rylan through, and then followed her inside. She parked and got out, her face brightening with awe.

Cole felt a swell of pride. They'd done a lot wrong when it came to opening the ranch as a tourist hot spot. But the one thing they'd done right was creating four permanent luxury tents that offered a posh alternative to camping, yet gave patrons the privacy and nature experience they craved. The tents had a one-year waiting list, and with people calling so often to reserve them, they were thinking about putting up more. The stark white tents were set forty feet apart against a backdrop of young trees and a wide creek,

"This place keeps getting more amazing." Rylan turned wonder-filled eyes on him. Cole paused from lifting a box from his truck, lost in her appreciation. Each time he showed her something new, she lit up like that. In the three years he and Livy had been married, she'd never sparked up like that about anything on the ranch. Not once. It took bank statements to make Livy come alive.

Brushing off the thought and focusing on the task at hand, Cole hefted boxes out of the back of his truck and made a neat row. "That's the butler house." He nodded to a stone building near the gate. "It'll be staffed twenty-four hours a day while the wedding party is here." Cole walked her to the closest tent.

Supported by a rustic log frame, the white canvas

structure sat on a raised wooden platform that was wide enough to offer a small deck area. Rylan followed Cole inside, her breath coming out in a rush. He hadn't been inside one of these in a while—it was stunning, yet somehow he'd forgotten. The interior was large enough for a king-size bed, dresser and nightstand, and a small round table and chairs, all made from hand-carved logs. A small en suite bathroom was resplendent in colored river stone and wood, the mirror framed in antlers. A hand-braided red-and-brown runner went from the bathroom to the bed, a coordinated rug at the entrance. Everything screamed luxury—from the antique trunk in the corner to the chandelier made from deer antlers hanging from the ceiling.

"Every tent is fully electric and has indoor plumbing. Five hundred square feet of easy money," Cole quipped, hands in his front pockets. Rylan glanced at him over her shoulder.

"Why do you say that?" She wandered around the bed. Cole tracked her fingers sliding along the log frame of the footboard.

"Rich people spare no expense. We charge more to host exclusive events, like this wedding, and they really don't care."

Rylan scoffed and peeked inside the bathroom. "My wedding cost five thousand dollars and I thought that was a lot." She dipped her head as though she couldn't believe that just came out of her mouth. He couldn't either. She was quiet, introspective, and though he shouldn't care—really, really shouldn't care—if she was going to talk about herself, he was all ears.

"Can't even rent these tents for that."

Rylan turned. "I was brought up not to waste money. Peter wanted a big, expensive event, but to me, it was too much. So, I kept it simple." He scanned her worn clothes and beat-up leather sandals. Rylan didn't scream "big spender," that was true…and refreshing.

"Divorced?" he asked casually.

She paused, her gaze everywhere but on him. "Widowed, actually." Well, hell. He hadn't been expecting that. Unease stabbed him beneath the ribs. Before he could think of an appropriate response, his cell phone went haywire in his pocket. He grabbed it, flipped it open.

"You?"

He looked up from the rapid-fire list of text messages that had just come in. "Me?"

She nodded, arms crossing over her breasts.

"Ah…divorced." Discussing his failed marriage was the last thing he had time for. Cole walked out onto the deck, eyes on his phone. Why people insisted on sending messages instead of just calling, made him want to throw the phone. Rylan stepped out onto the deck behind him.

"How…did your husband pass? I mean, you're so young," he said as he scanned the messages.

"Car accident." Her voice was emotionless, edged in stone. He looked up, his chest tugging for her. He and Livy had parted bitterly, but he couldn't imagine what it would have been like to lose her to an accident in their early years—when he'd loved her and thought she'd loved him. How wrong he'd been.

"Sorry to hear it."

"Don't be." Her voice kept its neutral tone, but it was edged with razors that time. In that way that she had, Rylan had just put him in his place again. He flipped through the messages, cutting off his ties to the conversation, and putting himself back into boss mode.

"So, these boxes are marked one through four. They are for the corresponding tents. One is on the far left, and then the numbers go up as you work your way down the row. Quilts, accessories, towels, linens, et cetera. All the things you need to make them homey and pretty." He gave her a nod and walked to his truck. She followed him.

"But—"

"Follow the diagram I gave you. And use your imagination. Just make it look good. Celebrities like things that look expensive, so just do that. It'll be fine." He slid inside the truck. "Lunch is being brought in by the wedding planner as a thank-you or something, so don't worry about cooking. Come up at noon. No household chores for you today—just focus on getting these tents done."

He pulled around to the gate, drove through, then got out to close it. Rylan was still standing there, arms crossed, looking after him.

"Problem?" he called. She didn't answer, but he saw the shake of her head right before she turned to the boxes. Good. She was doing what he'd told her to, and he was back to work, just as it should be.

Chapter Seven

Rylan walked into the ranch house laundry room to find a handful of very tiny kittens sleeping in a basket of washed and folded laundry. She looked around for Birdie, pretty sure no one else would put newborn kittens in a place like that. The shock of seeing them there only fueled her exhaustion. Preparing the tents had taken all day. She'd worked through the cool morning to the blaring noon heat to the tepid breeze of midday. After struggling with making the first tent "pretty," she'd gotten the hang of it, arranging and organizing accessories and essentials. She'd had to give herself a mental pat on the back. After being afraid she didn't have what it took to do the job, the tents had turned out amazing.

"I got kitties…" Birdie's shy voice tugged Rylan's attention. The child appeared in the doorway and eyed her from the frame, pointing at the basket. Rylan gripped her hip with one hand, digging fingers into her flesh and bone, as a tornado of unrest and sadness flared at seeing the little girl's face. Birdie's innocent kitty-bed-making was just childhood play—something Rachel might have done, too. Something Rachel would never do. It was so easy to see her lost child in Birdie. A stronger woman might have relished it, but Rylan wasn't sure she'd ever be strong enough for that.

"They were in the barn." Birdie came in one step. "They're brown and white and there's a black one." She pointed again, watching Rylan for a reaction. Rylan knew she should pick up the kittens and make a show of giving them hugs and kisses. Her focus shifted to the probability that the cats had probably peed everywhere and the laundry had to be redone. If she forced her brain to think about work, about redoing the laundry, it was easier not to think about Rachel.

She inhaled deeply through her nose and grabbed an empty cardboard box. Birdie watched her every move with her huge, beautiful ocean-green eyes. Her pink mouth bowed as Rylan gently put the kittens in the box. Birdie looked so much like Cole, it hurt. To think that beautiful man produced a gorgeous child like this and she had nothing.

"You're waking them up," Birdie protested. The disappointment in her voice cut Rylan deep. She shuddered, her heart leaden with agony as the kittens began to mewl. *Take it slow. It's not her fault Rachel is gone.*

"I'm sorry, but no cats on the laundry, Birdie." She looked around. "Where's the mama cat?"

"Barn." Birdie sucked her thumb, the bright light in her eyes dimmer. Rylan put the box on her hip and shooed Birdie out into the hall.

"You can't take babies away from their mom, Birdie," she said more harshly than she'd intended. Softer, she explained, "They need to be with their mama to eat and stay safe, okay?" Birdie let Rylan pass, and followed her out to the barn. The mama cat burst from a hay pile the moment she heard the kittens mewing. An anxious mother, Rylan thought, desperate for her babies. Only the mother cat got her babies back.

"Don't take the babies away again, Birdie. All right?"

Birdie's chin tipped to her chest, her thumb and forefinger pulling on her lower lip. "I wanted to show you my kitties." Birdie hiccupped, and Rylan's heart went through the meat grinder for a second time.

Rylan swallowed hard, heart racing. Then, tentatively, she held her hand out toward Birdie. She couldn't look, just focused on the kittens nursing from their mama. Small, warm fingers looped around her pinky and Rylan's rib cage bottomed out. Anguish quickly spilled into something else... something lighter. The tension in her chest loosened a little.

Birdie continued pulling her lip as they walked back down the dirt drive to the house. Cole came around on his horse, eyes going wide at seeing them. Birdie spotted him, pulled free from Rylan, and ran to him, bursting into tears. Cole reached down with one hand and picked his daughter up into the saddle, looking at Rylan with concern as Birdie cried into his shoulder.

Rylan hugged herself, cold despite the warmth of the late afternoon. Cole looked impressive on his big brown quarter horse, light-tan chaps snug over the length of his legs. His hat sat slightly askew so the curls showed above his ear.

"What's wrong?" Cole asked Birdie soothingly, looking at Rylan again. Birdie pulled him down to whisper in his ear. "She didn't like your kittens?" he asked gently as Birdie's sobbing and head shaking got worse.

A little breathless, Rylan held back the sting of threatened tears in her eyes. "I didn't mean to hurt her feelings — "

His eyes narrowed and took on an icy expression that forced shivers down her spine. Without a word to her, Cole nudged the horse and trotted off, Birdie curled up against his stomach and clinging to his shirt. Rylan watched them go, wondering how she'd screwed that up so badly. Her pinky burned from Birdie's touch. She flexed her fingers and slid them into the front pocket of her jeans. Learning how to endure Birdie's presence without turning into a mess of emotions was pretty critical to her mental health, and after the look on Cole's face, likely her job, too. But could she do that and still hang on to Rachel's memory? Rylan let the tears fall. She had to, because she wasn't ever going to let go.

• • •

"Mail." Tucker handed Cole a stack of envelopes and took a seat in a leather chair on the other side of the desk. Cole took them, threw them down, and finished typing on his laptop. Guests had started to arrive earlier in the evening for tomorrow's big wedding. The ranch was buzzing and he was wound tight, his brain spinning with everything left undone from his mental to-do list. A crack and fizz preceded the tasty scent of cold beer, prompting him to take notice. Tucker winked and chewed a toothpick, sliding Cole the beer before cracking open another.

"Anything from Levi?" Cole wasn't ashamed of the hope in his voice. He missed the hell out of his youngest brother. Each day Levi stayed in Afghanistan was one day too damn long.

"No." Tucker's disappointment matched his own. "Sure is hopping around here." Tuck plopped his feet on the edge of Cole's desk. "Good thing Ma has help this year. She's looking pretty run-down."

"Yeah." Maeve was looking more fatigued with each day, but she kept going despite protests from her children. Cole tried to convince her to see her doctor, but she insisted it could wait until after the celebrity wedding passed.

"Rylan's working her ass off," Tucker said behind a sip.

"Mmm-hmm." Cole shrugged and closed the laptop. She was supposed to work her ass off. That's what they paid her to do. Though he had to admit she was doing a hell of a good job. The house was spotless, the laundry was always done, and she cooked like a pro. Plus, she'd filled in to help with the wedding preparations without batting too much of an eye. He knew she'd cleaned up the kitchen and folded Birdie's laundry after working in the tents all day yesterday, too. She hadn't come up for lunch as he'd told her to either—hell, he wasn't sure she ever ate at all.

That thought made him pause. Guilt had been nagging him since he'd ridden off with Birdie. He shouldn't have stormed off like that, but he had a hard time being objective where his daughter was concerned. He'd been quick to assume Rylan had done something horrible to hurt Birdie's feelings. Though after Birdie admitted she'd put newborn kittens in the clean laundry, he could understand why Rylan wouldn't be overjoyed. He really needed to talk to her, smooth things over.

Tucker was eyeballing him in that frustrating Tucker way—as though he had something to say but couldn't bring himself to let it out.

Cole sighed impatiently and leaned back in his chair. "Spit it out, Tuck."

"Ma seems to like her." Tucker clicked the tab on his beer can.

Cole rubbed a hand over his face, knowing damn well that wasn't really what Tucker had on his mind. "Ma also takes in three-legged horses and rabid raccoons." She had a knack for picking up offbeat strays and trying her best to make something useful from them. It didn't usually work out that well. "Ma likes everyone."

Tucker sat forward in his chair and leaned his forearms on the desk. "You think Rylan's in some kind of trouble?"

Cole set his beer down, his brows arching at the question. Tucker was the family watchdog and made no qualms about voicing his opinion when he thought something, or someone, was bad for the family or the ranch. Tucker tapped on the letters.

Cole picked up the two envelopes, both addressed to Rylan, both from a legal office in Wisconsin. After her strange reaction to Birdie and her avoidance of family in general, he'd wondered what she might be hiding, too, hadn't he? Cole shook his head. He didn't want to worry about whether or not Rylan was a deviant. Her background check came out clean. She'd been a cop, for crying out loud. If they couldn't trust someone with an impeccable police service record, the world really was going to shit. So far, he had no reason not to trust her as an employee with his home and his family.

Despite the way his mind loved to wander in her general direction for no good reason, maybe he *should* consider her a deviant. If he focused on all the things Rylan might be, maybe he'd stop thinking about the things she was. Sexy. Smoky. Curvy. Women as employees? Fine. Women after his heart? No way.

"Just say whatever is rolling around in that thick skull of yours, Tucker."

Tucker flicked the toothpick from one side of his mouth to the other. "I'm saying you already got involved with the wrong woman once, who also happened to work here. We can't afford for you to do it again."

"Whoa. Hold the fuck on." Cole leaned forward so fast, his chair squeaked like a cracking tree. His fists curled right next to Tucker's hands on the walnut desk. He and Tucker were close. Having gone through the brunt of their father's hostility growing up, they'd learned that sticking together made it easier to handle whatever shit got flung at them. Tucker had been there when Livy showed her true colors, had helped Cole through it. He couldn't blame Tucker for not wanting to go down that road again.

Cole knew he sure as hell couldn't do it again. Which is why Rylan was fun to look at but dangerous to play with. He would've thought Tuck knew that already.

"I'm not interested in her."

Tucker faced him squarely with a clear I-don't-believe-you wink. "Fine, but if you decide to *get* interested just… Have a good time, but don't get attached."

Cole scoffed. "Just love 'em and leave 'em like you do, huh?" As soon as he said the words, Cole regretted them. Tucker had been burned once, too. Hell, they even stuck together in heartbreak. "I'm sorry, Tuck. Forget I said that."

"Asshole." A slow, crooked grin spread on Tucker's mouth.

"Mostly, yeah." Cole knocked his brother's fist with his own.

Tucker resumed his beer drinking and got quiet again, which only raised Cole's suspicions. "Is there more?" He kept his arms on the desk, pretty sure by the squint of Tucker's left eye that he wasn't going to like what was coming next.

"Speaking of Livy—"

"Fuck," Cole groaned, closing his eyes. Nope, he wasn't going to like it.

"She called the house. You're damn lucky I happened to be there when the phone rang, and not Ma." Tucker got up, crushed his can in one hand and tossed it in the wastebasket. Cole got up too, simply because every muscle in his body was screaming that he needed to hit something.

"What the hell did she want?"

Tucker shrugged. "I don't know, but she did say that if you don't call her soon, she's coming out here. Spare us her presence, Cole. Call. Her. Back."

Call Livy back. Doing just that had been nagging him since she'd started hounding him two weeks ago. He'd given Livy exactly what she wanted when they parted ways and took away the one thing she'd never get back: Birdie. In the back of his mind, he had wondered if Livy would pop back up at some point and what she'd want if she did.

He knew only one thing—she'd never get her fake nails on his daughter again.

"I'll take care of it," Cole grumbled, grabbing the letters off the desk and walking to the door. "Birdie's in bed. You staying inside?" he called back to Tucker.

"I'll keep an eye on Sleeping Beauty. You go blow off some steam."

Cole walked to Rylan's room, tapping the envelopes against his palm. He struggled with the desire to ask her what they were about—knew he had no right—and wrestled with himself to just shut up when she answered the door. Another knock later, she still hadn't answered. It was nine thirty, and he doubted she was sleeping. He cranked the handle, his heart kicking up. It was unlocked.

"Rylan?" he called through the crack, opening the door wide when no answer came. The room was empty. The space was tidy and completely without any of the personal touches he'd expected to see. No pictures or personal effects besides an iPad on the bedside table. Whatever her past held, she hadn't brought reminders of it with her. At least nothing she wanted anyone else to see. He set the letters on her pillow and stormed from the room, needing the space and comfort only the open air could bring him.

Out on the deck, he was met by the lively strains of fiddle. Each night during the summer, ranch guests were invited to a nightly campfire for s'mores and socializing. Some of the ranch hands would come by and tell stories or scare the kids with ghost tales. Cole usually had nothing to do with it, but the music tonight called to him. Some of the tension inside faded as the fiddle sped up, followed by a banjo. He meandered toward the guest cabins, a vibrant orange glow welcoming him from the fire. The log benches situated around the huge fire ring were packed with guests. Long sticks held sloppy, gooey marshmallows, and the rustle of candy wrappers betrayed that chocolate was near.

Jaxon, Zane, and Don—three of Paint River's cowboys—stood off to one side, Jaxon and Zane with their fiddles, Don with the banjo. The trio was unofficially called the Paint River Pickers, just three men who loved to play and took every opportunity to do so. The nightly campfire had become a preferred venue.

Cole paused mid-step when he saw Rylan. She was bustling around helping guests with their s'mores and collecting candy wrappers and trash in a little bag. Her red shirt was untucked, her hair pulled over her shoulder in a messy braid. It bothered him that she was still working when it was well past the time she should have been done for the day. He wanted to talk to her about the Birdie-kitten incident anyway. Maybe he could get her to rest a minute in the process. Her back was to him when he started her way.

"Cole!" He glanced around for the source of his name and was surprised to see his mother sitting across the fire, her arm looped through a man's. He tilted his head to see who she was with, recognizing Jim Gilfoyle, a longtime family friend. A famous novelist, Gilfoyle spent three months of the summer in a private cabin on the property and had been like a surrogate uncle to the Haywood boys for as long as Cole could remember. He must have arrived sometime earlier that day, and given the huge grin on his mom's face, she was pretty glad to have her friend around. He gave his mom a nod and resumed his path, intent on getting to Rylan.

"Play me something!" Maeve called out. No sooner had she said the words than Jaxon was next to him, thrusting a fiddle into his hands.

The cowboy tipped his hat back and waggled his eyebrows. "Play for your mama." Cole was tempted to give the fiddle back; he hadn't played since before Birdie was born. There had to be thirty people sitting around the fire, but it *had* been a while, and hell, why not…

Jaxon raised his own fiddle to his chin and pulled a few introductory chords. Cole tipped his head back with a smile and a nod at the familiar notes. He watched his mother's face burst into a smile, her hands eagerly waving Rylan over to sit down. His chest welled, sudden nerves making his skin prickly.

Rylan would be watching.

Cole put the fiddle into position and pulled the bow a few times, his brain and fingers immediately in sync as if he'd been playing faithfully all these years. He dared one quick look at Rylan. Her elbows were on her knees, hands cupped together, eyes fixed on him. He looked down at the strings, repositioned the bow, and pulled it in quick succession to start the first three cords. Once that little bit filled the air, excitement from the music's promise flowed through him.

"'Morrison's Jig,' everyone!" Jaxon introduced. Strongly Irish, it was Maeve's favorite song, and she wasn't shy about poking her boys to play it once in a while. Fast and vibrant with complicated finger placement, it demanded perfect bow control and had taken Cole a year to learn to play flawlessly. Despite his not playing for so long, the song came to life on its own, filling the air with full-bodied Irish cheer. The timbre pounded his soul and reverberated into his core. The fiddle sat perfectly on his shoulder, the weight welcome and familiar. Damn if that didn't feel good.

Evenly paced in the beginning, "Morrison's Jig" birthed a strain that compelled people to tap their feet or move in some way. It couldn't be helped—the song demanded it.

Low chords, high chords, and a blend of sounds in between revved up the soul. The music beat within him, washing away everything that had been wrong that day, replacing it with pure, high elation. He smiled, feeling it in his entire body.

He suddenly stopped playing and held the bow above the strings, heard the soft murmuring of people wondering if it was over. Then he smiled wider, swung to the left, and started playing again doubly fast, drawing the tones and chords so rapidly that people cheered and leaped to their feet. Zane tapped on a log in accompaniment.

It was a whirlwind of music, and it consumed him. Sneaking a look at Rylan, he saw an expression of pure joy and wonderment on her face. Firelight flickered across her hair as she tapped her foot to the music. Patrons were hopping and dancing around her, but she sat, absorbing everything, enjoying it all. Cole had the urge to drop the damn fiddle and run over to her, scoop her off the bench, and carry her off somewhere.

His wrist and fingers were burning, but he kept it going, pulling the tones round and round as fast as he dared without losing the song's substance, until he reached the end and raised the bow and fiddle high. The cheering and whooping made his face flush, but his heart raced with exhilaration. Good old Irish fiddle, he thought. Nothing like it.

Cole handed Zane the fiddle, and the trio immediately dived into a new set.

"Come sit," Maeve called to him. Cole greeted Jim and Rylan as he walked over, flushed when Maeve took his hand and gave it a joyful squeeze. Cole lifted his mother's hand to his lips, gave her a kiss and a squeeze back. He was hyper-aware of Rylan sitting near his right leg. Her face tipped up to catch his eyes, her cheeks flushed a soft pink.

"I don't have words for how amazing that was," she said. The urge to carry her off got worse, only now he was imagining hauling her away caveman-style. Over his shoulder with her ass in the air.

Maeve patted Rylan's arm. "He's one of the best fiddlers I've ever heard, and I grew up with a whole lot of 'em. Natural talent. He takes after my dad, Paddy McBannon."

"True talent." Rylan placed one graceful hand over her heart. "It made my chest thump!"

Cole dipped his head and smiled. Her compliment spread over him like warm honey, and it was unnerving. He cared way too much that she'd liked his set. "Fiddle will do that to you."

Jim leaned over with a smile and grabbed Cole's hand for a hearty shake. "What did your daddy say, Maeve?" He cleared his throat a couple times and dug up an Irish accent. "Me tinks me garrl fell from da heavens. Only arhn angel can 'ave eyes dat blue."

The fire snapped and cracked to his mother's laughter. Cole sat back on the log, some of his fiddle euphoria fading off. Maeve slid her arm around Jim's shoulder as they laughed. Rylan encouraged Jim to keep talking with his good old brogue. What was this? Cole shuffled his boot in the dirt. They were laughing, teasing, carrying on like…like the Haywoods used to years ago.

Before his brother left for the Marines. Before his wife took his money and ran. Before his asshole father died.

"Did you hear me?" Rylan was looking at him, her skin cast gold in the firelight. He blinked slowly just to take her all in. Her eyes were wide and dark, cheekbones swathed in shadow, her lips tantalizing in the flickering glow. Cole's eyes fell to her neck, to the open top buttons of her shirt and the material capturing her breasts just right. His jeans got uncomfortably tight as he imagined cupping them in his hands.

"Hmm?" His gaze snapped back to hers. Shit, she looked beautiful.

"I asked how long you've been playing. You're exceptional."

Exceptional? Decent, at best. At least, that's how Livy had made him feel about it. She'd hated the fiddle, hated it when he'd played. So he'd put the instrument away, for her. "Ma started me out when I was seven."

It was unsettling to have her eyes on him like this. "I hope you'll play again soon." She stood, stretching her back so her breasts leaned into the fabric. Turning to Maeve and Jim, she excused herself. Cole took two big steps to Rylan's side.

"I'll walk you back." Before he could think, he put a hand to her lower back and guided her around the log bench. He almost faltered from the soft, warm impact of her body on his palm but maintained his stride. She tensed briefly under his touch, and he felt a little shiver shake her body. Cold? No way. It had to be at least seventy degrees out still. The thought that his touch made her react that way bolstered the feeling that this was right.

That being next to her felt so good.

That touching her felt so right.

The fiddle and banjo serenaded them away from the campfire. She glanced at him once as they crossed the yard but didn't speak. They climbed the stairs on the side of the deck, Rylan two steps ahead of him, her brown braid swaying along her back. He had a bracing urge to undo the strands and run his fingers through them. She paused at the top of the steps, leaning her hip against the railing under the soft porch light. Cole stopped beside her, realizing how easy it would be to put a hand on either side of the railing and trap her between his arms. Then he could press against her and feel those perfect breasts against his chest. Her lips would be soft, her mouth hot and wet when he kissed her and plunged his tongue inside, crushing her against him and driving his hips against her…

She eyed him shyly as she stepped away, almost as if she knew what he was thinking, her fingers running along the smooth wooden railing until they slid off the edge. Cole reached out and caught her hand before it could fall to her side. Her fingers curled around his palm at the same time she drew a quick breath. His thumb swept the back of her hand before he entwined his fingers softly with hers.

Rylan tipped her chin up, moonlight highlighting the flush on her cheeks and the plump, delicious promise of her mouth. A mouth that parted just a fraction before she sucked her lower lip in and worried it between her teeth. Her fingers clenched and released around his. Cole watched her intently as he rubbed his thumb in small circles over her soft palm. A tremor went through her, and his heart swelled.

Her eyes flashed silver, and Cole's breath hitched as he pressed his torso against hers. God, he could lose himself in those eyes. The soft mounds of her breasts sank against him, raising a hot, steady flush over his forearms and down his spine, straight to his groin. He wanted to kiss her senseless, watch those beautiful eyes close in a clench of passion.

Before he could rationalize all the reasons not to, Cole wrapped a hand around the back of Rylan's neck, the other sliding around the feminine curve of her waist. Her arms hung loose at her sides, her spine stiffening as he dipped his head low so her breath washed over his lips, hot and moist and sweet, like peppermint. Rylan sucked in a shaky breath, her hands coming up to gently, tentatively, grasp his sides. She fisted his shirt, her neck becoming pliable as he urged her head back just a touch. Fire burned his skin beneath the weight of her hands, urging Cole to take what he wanted. And oh, he wanted to. So badly.

Rylan's chest heaved. A soft, needy exclamation escaped her lips. Shit, she wanted it too. With a muttered curse, Cole claimed her mouth, his lips brushing hers in a barely there kiss that had enough power to rivet him to the porch. Rylan pulled him closer, her body arching into him as her lips parted under his. He met her mouth with a hard, open kiss that punched him in the brain, threatened to pull the plug on his restraint.

"Oh, God." Rylan's husky, pleasure-filled voice hit him like a slap. Cole jerked. What the hell was he doing? He pulled back, surprised to see his hands trembling. Rylan sank back against the railing behind her, both her hands going out to grip it like a lifeline. Her expression was equally surprised and sensual with a heavy dose of doe-in-the-headlights swirled in.

Cole pressed the heel of his palm to his lips. For fuck's sake, he was making out with the housekeeper. The very hot, very tempting housekeeper. He'd only barely sampled her flesh, but her taste was round and bold on his lips, promising so much more if he'd just dive back in. He couldn't. Cole backed away as Rylan's eyes changed from light silver to storm gray.

He turned away, so angry with himself and so aroused by her that he could barely form words. An apology was in order—but he wasn't sorry. How could he be sorry when holding her, tasting her, was perfect? He might not want to regret it, but he probably would if he didn't get a rein on his testosterone.

"Good night, Rylan." Cole stormed toward the French doors to put distance between them before he went back to finish what he started or she pounced him like an angry cat. He couldn't help thinking it would be win-win either way.

"Hey!" Rylan's voice stopped him before he went inside. The door lever bit into his palm when he gripped it hard. Her sandals made a scuffing sound across the deck planks as she came closer. "Maybe instead of running away, you could just talk to me."

A muscle twitched in his cheek. He shouldn't engage in this conversation with her. He had kissed her. He shouldn't have, and it wouldn't happen again. End. Of. Story.

She cocked her head when he didn't say anything. "Your daughter gets upset with me, but instead of asking me what happened, you glare and ride off. And now you kiss me, and then jerk away like—"

"I'm sorry about Birdie. I overreacted."

Rylan rocked back on her heels just a bit. "Oh." The utterance was soft, as if he'd taken her off guard. "Thank you. I—I truly didn't mean to hurt her feelings." Her honest reactions to everything killed him. She was raw and unabashed, and he wished, for one damn day, he could live that authentically. But he didn't dare make himself vulnerable again.

He opened the door and gave her one last look. "The kiss was a mistake."

"Right." Her voice wavered, challenging the truth in his statement as he slipped inside and shut the door. Dammit, it wasn't a mistake. His heart knew it well...which meant he was headed for deep shit.

Chapter Eight

Rylan was up and off for a run at daybreak. Restless the night before, she felt like she'd barely slept a wink. Cole's kiss was a permanent imprint on her lips, his taste and the sensation of his mouth on hers on constant replay in her brain. Each time she savored the memory, her body lit with a desire she hadn't experienced in…forever. It had been so long since she'd been with a man—since she'd *wanted* to be with a man—each new flicker of yearning created by the memory of Cole's kiss set off a demanding thrum through her blood.

His mouth and his performance on the fiddle had left her awestruck. Tall and lean, broad-shouldered with biceps bulging beneath his dark shirt as he held the fiddle under his chin, he'd looked wild and alive. The top buttons of his shirt were undone, showing off a patch of gleaming skin and dark hair. His thighs firm and legs wide as he'd commanded the music. Hat tipped back, his blue eyes had flashed when he saw how the music captured the crowd. Sexy didn't even begin to describe how Cole Haywood had looked last night.

She'd tossed and turned most of the night, imagining all the ways she could have a super-orgasm with a man like that on top of her. It was the music—she was sure of it. He'd gotten caught up in it himself and took it out on her. Not that she was complaining. Though she probably should be. One minute he had been watching her with an expression she'd never seen on a man's face where she was concerned: unabashed want. And the next he had been scowling at her.

The house was quiet when she got back from running and started to brew a pot of coffee. Sweaty and starving, she downed some toast and let her body temperature regulate by walking through the living room and tidying up. She collected hampers and grabbed the dirty towels from the bathroom. With guests arriving last night and the celebrity wedding going on later today, Rylan wanted to help out as much as possible. She'd seen the to-do list for odds and ends that needed to be completed. It was enough to make Rylan's inner workhorse have a heart attack. Most of the tasks were for Cole and Tucker, though Maeve had a few things she'd hoped to do. When Maeve had come in from the campfire last night, pale and trembling, it was obvious her health wasn't going to allow it. Tucker had given her a handful of pills and helped her to bed. Right then she'd known Maeve needed more help than she let on.

Wanting to get the housework done fast so she could offer to lend a hand, Rylan stepped into the laundry room and stopped dead to see Cole standing at the washer in nothing but white briefs and his battered cowboy hat. His muscular arms bunched as he threw laundry into the machine, the curve of his back, and the round, firm mounds of his ass covered in stretched white cotton. The luscious view did little to curb the longing that had nagged her all night.

"You can close your mouth," he whispered. "A cowboy doing laundry isn't that uncommon." Rylan didn't trust herself to speak. Cole started the machine and proceeded to take a load out of the dryer, each bend and movement of his body showing off the strong glide of muscle under supple skin. He snapped a pair of jeans, slid one leg in, then another. Her libido jacked with each delicious movement.

Just throw me on the washer and pound me senseless so I can get over it.

"I'm sorry," she said. "If you want to put your laundry outside your door, I'll—"

His voice was light. "I don't need you doing my damn laundry."

"Oh" was all she could manage to say. Cole gathered a bundle of clothes in one arm. He looked sideways at her, long and hard. If words were visible, she was sure there would be some hanging from his mouth, but he didn't let them out. Rylan hitched the laundry basket in her arms to her hip. The lust-fueled haze in her brain tiptoed reluctantly away. *Work. Focus on work.*

"May I ask you something?"

His eyes fell to her lips, his arm tightening around the bundle of laundry in the crook of his elbow. "Sure."

She paused, knowing it was none of her business but needing to ask anyway. "What's wrong with Maeve? I mean, I've seen the calluses on her hands; I know she's worked hard. And to see her so weak… It breaks my heart."

"She hasn't told you? Figures. She's still in a state of denial about it…" He paused. "Wait. It breaks your heart? You barely know her." A small line appeared between his eyes.

Rylan slid a hand over her chest with a nod. "I do know her. She makes it easy." The sudden heaviness was hard to hold back. She'd grown up motherless, something she shared with Birdie. When she was younger and had imagined what her mom might be like, a hardworking country woman like Maeve was pretty close to her childhood fantasy. Cole was watching her while she tried to rope in fast tears. She hated that he saw. *Weakling.* For years, no one had been privy to her inner emotions. She was an expert at holding them in — or had been until Paint River. Ever since she'd gotten here, all the feelings just came out whenever the hell they wanted to.

His tempting lips pulled into a sympathetic line. "Ma does have that effect on people. She's been through a lot but has never lost her warm heart." He was pretty perceptive for a man who liked to play the hard-ass. She wondered just how many layers Cole had underneath his rough attitude — she wanted to find out more than she wanted to admit.

The pad of his thumb rested against his lips for a moment. "Ma has multiple sclerosis. That's why she trembles and gets weak. Some days are really bad, other days she's almost like her old self. She had symptoms for about five years before she ever told anyone. By the time we finally got her to agree to testing, she had severe symptoms. Falling over. Had to stay in bed for days sometimes."

Rylan crossed her arms and leaned against the doorframe. "Tucker said she wasn't doing well after the bonfire last night and that she should stay in bed." Quiet sadness played over his face and Rylan realized just how devastating his mother's illness was for him. Such little displays of emotion leaked out of him when he probably had no idea they did. Her heart warmed. Cole Haywood, it seemed, was a very loving man under all that tough armor.

"Yeah, she should. The medication should help her sleep most of the morning. I'm taking Birdie to my aunt's house for the weekend, so Ma doesn't have to worry about watching her." The deep tone to his voice made heat spread through her torso and right out to her fingertips. He shifted a little, bringing his bare chest inches from her hands. Rylan couldn't help but glance over his wide, perfect muscles. He caught her looking and his resulting smile wasn't just wicked—it was bone-busting lust married to evil. Silence dropped between them, their gazes tangling.

Cole tapped his lip with his thumb, seeming to contemplate a minute. "About last night—"

She didn't hesitate. "You already said it was a mistake. Noted." How could he think it had been wrong when his perfect mouth had made her feel…alive? His chin tilted up, his eyes bright with an expression she couldn't read. He leaned in, the heat from his chest wafting across her bare forearms as he slid sideways out the door.

"Let's stop while we're ahead, before we're both sorry," he said. "Agreed?"

Bricks tumbled down inside her. Playing with fire and all that. "Absolutely." Rylan's resolve turned to steel, years of learning how to barricade her inner self from the outside world coming into play. "Have a good day, M—"

"Don't." Cole gave her a half-assed glance. He looked as

though he was going to say more, his voice cutting off with a jolt to the sound of Birdie screaming. He dropped the laundry and hurried out into the hall. Rylan followed him, both of them stopping at the base of the stairs as Birdie came racing down, one hand over her head with blood seeping through her tiny fingers.

Panic welled in Cole so hard and fast he had to put one hand on the wall to steady himself. He could handle a lot of shit, but seeing Birdie hurt wasn't on that list. Her blood matting her white-blond hair and covering the front of her purple nightgown very nearly brought him to his knees. Birdie getting hurt—Birdie being ripped away from him—were his biggest fears. Every drop of blood posed a threat.

He reached for her as she cleared the last step. "What happened?" Sweat broke out along his hairline.

Instead of running into his arms, Birdie ran past him, gripped the hem of Rylan's shirt and wailed harder. Rylan stood like a statue, arms splayed wide, complete shock on her face. She met Cole's eyes, her lips parted for a moment before she snapped out of it. Something crossed her face, urgent and full of concern. It was the same look he'd seen on his mother's face when he or one of his brothers would come in with an injury—the need to make it better. She gave him a questioning look as her hands closed over Birdie's back in a comforting cross. Cole nodded, a flutter of relief going through him that Rylan would deal with the blood, that she'd make Birdie better.

Rylan hefted Birdie onto her hip and rushed her into

the hallway bathroom. Setting her on the sink, she smoothed back what she could of Birdie's hair. Cole stood on Birdie's other side, hating that he felt so out of control and useless. He'd raised Birdie since she was an infant; he knew how to care for her better than anyone. Except for times like this. Maeve always stepped in when Birdie was hurt, and now, Rylan. He cupped his daughter's chin and ushered her hand down. A small laceration marred the flesh on her right temple.

"What happened, baby?"

"I...fell!"

Rylan wet a washcloth and held it to Birdie's forehead. Cole dug in the cupboard for a bandage and some antibacterial cream, his heart upping a thousand notches at the smooth, sympathetic expression on Rylan's face. Her hand trembled slightly as she held the washcloth, but her tender touch didn't go unnoticed.

"Did you roll out of bed again?" Cole held the rest of Birdie's tangled blond curls out of the way as Rylan cleaned the wound. Birdie hiccupped between sobs, her lower lip quivering as she nodded. Guilt stabbed him at having taken the safety rail off her bed after she begged him to let her be a "big girl." She'd rolled out twice now. That damn rail was going back on. Today.

"Ry, I hit my table."

Ry? Cole's eyebrows went up. Looked like he was being bypassed in the conversation. Rylan put a little cream on a cotton swab and dabbed it on the cut. Birdie kicked her legs as her sobbing grew quieter.

Rylan's voice was soft and soothing. "You did? That darn table."

Birdie looked at Rylan with huge, watery eyes. Her downtrodden expression punched Cole in the gut. She sniffed. "I hate that table."

Rylan opened the bandage, frowning in agreement. Her hands were still shaking. "I hate that table, too, Birdie." Cole's skin pebbled with goose bumps at the sound of Rylan wetting the cloth again, and the soft slide of the terry cloth across Birdie's skin and hair as she wiped the remaining blood away. The gentle tones of her voice as she told Birdie she was good as new made him feel light yet heavy at the same time.

The scene shouldn't have looked so natural, so *right*, but it did. Rylan helped Birdie down with a reassuring, albeit quick, pat on the head. The knot in his gut was gone, filled with relief that it had been nothing more than a little cut. Birdie wrapped her arms around his leg, and he picked her up, held her tight. Damn head wounds. They always bled more than anything and he knew that. But he still couldn't stop the worry that something horrible would happen to his Birdie.

"You okay, baby?" He kissed her cheek. Birdie shook her head and buried her face in his neck.

"No shirt, Daddy." Her little fingers toyed with his hair, her nose pressed into the bare curve of his neck and shoulder. Cole laughed and patted her back.

"I was getting dressed when I heard you crying." He swung around to face Rylan. She stopped cleaning up the mess on the sink to look at him. The urge to pull her in and kiss her was so strong Cole had to take a step back to stop himself from doing it.

"Thank you," he said softly. Maybe too softly. It was a

cop-out to thank her when she might not even hear it, but saying the words made Cole feel like he was taking one step closer to something he wouldn't be able to stop. Rylan gave a wan smile, and he knew she'd heard him. He took one more step back. "All right, baby. Let's get you ready to go to Auntie Penny's. If you get a headache or a sick tummy, you need to tell me right away, okay?"

Cole sucked in a deep breath, running through his mental to-do list at the same time his brain replayed how natural Rylan and Birdie had looked together—like a family. He shook it off as he climbed the stairs with Birdie on his hip. He'd told Rylan they would both be sorry if they gave in to this attraction between them, and he was sticking to it.

• • •

The catering truck got stuck in the mud, the gate on the henhouse broke allowing four dozen guinea fowl to run over the manicured lawn, and one of the dogs decided to kill a gopher and deposit the body in the catering tent. Cole managed to mend it all, only to have Pana Bar Noir kick out a panel in his stall. The horse was beautiful but more lunatic than sane and managed to slam Cole against the metal bars of the stall door, immediately setting Cole's ribs on fire.

Holding his agonized side and cursing a blue streak, he was more than happy when the wedding planners informed him they had everything under control. He loved that part—when the ranch was in order and the event people could do their thing. That meant he was off the hook...for a while. Cole limped into the house, ready to down some ibuprofen to kill the ache in his side.

But then he saw Rylan in the dining room, and the ache started again, only in a spot much lower than his ribs. She wore a gauzy pink dress, hemmed just above her knees with a sleeveless bodice hugging her full breasts. The back scooped low below the tie, showing off her firm back muscles and the curve of her spine. Rylan had her hair pulled to one side, the soft curls gleaming chestnut and red with streaks of sun-kissed blond. He must have groaned a little—at least he did in his mind—because she spun and dropped an earring she'd been holding. His gaze swept her from top to bottom and back up again, settling on her pink, glossy lips. Goddamn, she looked incredible.

"Hi." Her voice was breathy and rushed. "Are you all right? I heard you got slammed by a horse."

His forehead scrunched. Word traveled fast, apparently. "I was fine." Cole retrieved her earring and held it palm-out so her fingers traced his skin when she took it.

"Was?" She fingered a stray lock of hair away from her neck then fiddled with the earring. Dumbstruck didn't come close to how his brain was reacting.

"Hmm?"

Rylan laughed and smoothed the front of her dress, shifting uncomfortably. "You said you *were* feeling fine. So, you're not now?" How could she even ask him something like that? What man would feel fine standing next to her when she looked so elegant and sexy and completely strippable?

"Why so dressed up?" He avoided her question, hoping his body didn't give anything away. She looked down and swore when she noticed that one strappy, golden sandal had come unbuckled. She bent, her breasts mounding beautifully over the top of the bodice. Rylan quickly covered her chest with one arm and stood, a blush fanning her cheeks. Cole frowned, disappointed that the scenery had changed so fast.

"The wedding planner had an employee call in sick so she asked me to serve wine in the reception tent. Luckily your mom had this dress in her closet. Tags still on it."

His heart lurched with the realization that the dress was likely one Livy had left behind. But then Rylan pulled out a chair and crossed her graceful legs to strap the shoe and he forgot about the dress. Forgot about all the reasons he shouldn't be feeling the desire humming through him. It would be so easy to just—

Cole clamped his jaw, moved in front of her, and bent to one knee, ignoring the shot of pain that lanced through his side. "Put your foot up here." He reached for her calf. Rylan jerked at his touch but relented, letting him place her foot right above his knee. Cole grabbed the strap over her ankle, heat shooting through his groin when she shuddered. Her skin was freshly shaven and silky smooth, and it was all he could do to stop from running his fingers along the curve of her leg. She smelled amazing, her body heat against his fingers, intoxicating. It took a huge dose of concentration and some mental testosterone-stomping, but he got the shoe strapped and stepped back. Rylan cleared her throat and stood, the blush even deeper on her cheeks.

Jesus, he wanted to grab her against him and kiss her again. Deeper, hotter, longer than before. He should tell her she looked beautiful. He should tell her he wanted…

"Holy hell! Who exchanged the housekeeper for a supermodel?" Tucker came in from the hall, shirtless and freshly scrubbed. He gave Rylan a low whistle and stopped beside her with one leg hitched. "Damn, woman. You look incredible." Tuck unbundled the T-shirt in his hands and slid it on.

Cole squeezed his eyes shut. Yeah, he should have said that.

Rylan dipped her head. "Thanks."

"Walk you to the reception tent?" Tucker held a crooked arm to her, and Rylan paused, sneaking a quick glance at Cole. Tucker followed her gaze and lowered his arm slightly. Cole bit back anger—jealousy, if he were honest about it. He didn't have time to mess with this right now. Rylan looked beautiful. Tucker beat him to saying it. Fine. It shouldn't bother him if Tucker escorted Rylan to the tent, to the store, to his bed. She was the help. Never mind her sensuality, incredible work ethic, and caring soul that threatened to reel his heart in anyway. No way. There wasn't any room at the ranch for another heartbreak. No room, no emotional reserve, and damn well no money to pay for another big-ass mistake.

Before he could turn away, Tucker sidled up to him and grumbled into his ear. "I know you tried to deny it the other day, big brother, but the look on your face right now confirms that it's my turn to do this." Tucker slapped Cole on the chest with a raise of his eyebrows and whispered with animated emphasis, "Handbook."

Cole clenched his teeth to hold back both a smile and the left hook he was about to deliver to his brother's face. Instead, he turned and flipped Tucker off. "I'm outta here."

Rylan's soft sigh followed him out and damn if it didn't sound a little like disappointment.

Chapter Nine

Three in the morning finally saw an end to the drinking and dancing. Celebrities and their guests didn't much know when to call it a night, Rylan thought. Limos were hauling the ones who weren't staying on the ranch back to their hotel in nearby Missoula while the immediate wedding party settled into the luxury tents. She watched things settle down from the empty reception tent. A soft fiddle played in the background as Jaxon, Don, and Zane crafted a final slow tune. Rylan sat on a stool and let the music seep into her, wishing she could hear Cole play again.

Tucker had been by a while ago, holding a half-empty bottle of wine in one hand and a beer in the other. He'd handed her the wine with a wink. "Have some. It's good." And he'd left. She'd nursed the sweet, blackberry wine — at least, she thought she had. The warm buzz and hum in her veins told her maybe she hadn't been as prudent as she should have been. All day, she'd tried to forget how it had felt to care for Birdie that morning. Once the initial shock took a hike, pure motherly instinct had taken over. Fix it. Make it better. Kiss the boo-boo and dry the tears.

Birdie had turned to her, not Cole, a surprise that pulled Rylan's heartstrings so hard they nearly snapped. In a tiny, quiet way, it had felt amazingly good to be needed like that. To be wanted. When Birdie's small arms reached for her, Rylan nearly lost herself in the memory of another pair of small arms reaching for her in a time of pain or fear. She'd held Rachel countless times, dried her little tears, and this morning, for just a moment, she'd been a mother again. A gnarled web of emotion had rolled around in her brain—fear, joy, regret, longing—slinging arrows to her heart. Her child was gone, and she could not, would not, replace her.

No wonder the wine tasted so good.

Just when she considered it time to head inside, Rylan spotted Cole wandering into the tent, hands shoved in his front pockets. She boldly watched him come closer, her pulse getting quicker with each step he took. She wanted him. The bad-girl side of her said it was time to take a risk, to be up-front with him and see where it led. The rational side of her, the one that usually got its way in matters like this, said no way. So many things about Cole Haywood made him the type of man she'd always wanted: strong, hardworking, sexy, caring. His appeal was starting to override common sense, and she was just tempted enough to let her body overrule her head. Rylan narrowed her eyes and took another drink. *Ah, heck. Let the wine decide.*

Cole laughed as he sauntered over. Light-blue shirt half-unbuttoned. Snug, dark jeans, with a square silver belt buckle. And those eyes—the eyes that she could never get enough of—piercing right through her. She nibbled her lower lip, then gave a mock salute with a wine bottle. He strode over to her place on the stool and hitched a hip against the bar.

"That's Paint River's homemade wine. It's pretty strong. You'd better be careful with—" Cole's voice drifted off with a sigh when she showed him how little was left. "Did you drink the entire bottle?"

Rylan made a *pfft* sound. "What?" She gave a forced pout. "No…it was almost empty when Tucker gave it to me." For a fleeting second, she wondered if she'd get in trouble for drinking. "I figured he owns this place, too, so if he said to drink some wine, I'd drink some wine."

Emboldened by Cole's easy smile and the way he leaned a little closer to her, Rylan cocked her head and grabbed his gaze. He was gorgeous. It hurt the deepest pit of her stomach, made her chest hurt and her center ache, all with one glance. Ridiculous.

"You know, the first time I ever drank wine was at my wedding." Rylan set the bottle between her legs. The bunched, hiked skirt of her dress floated off the stool and brushed his knee in a reminder that only inches separated her long, bared legs from his body. He could reach out and touch her if he wanted to. *If.* Did he want to? God, did he?

She looked down at the bottle, rimmed the opening with her pinky. "I married Peter Donovan. *Judge* Donovan. Yeah. But he didn't want me. Not *me*, me, you know. Just the image. He figured marrying the hero cop would be good for his career." Her cheeks went hot as the words spilled out. Oh hell, what did it matter? There could never be anything between her and Cole—she was an emotionally broken housekeeper now, and being sued for every dime in her bank account and then some, thanks to the civil suit brought against her from the car accident her husband had caused.

Husband. What a joke.

Cole reached out and took the bottle from her, his hand brushing against her thigh. Dark curiosity flickered in his eyes, mixed with a little surprise. Her eyebrows rose. Well, why stop now? She had plenty more secrets. Rylan licked her lips, the sweet remnant taste of tangy wine on the tip of her tongue. Leave it to a little alcohol to give her a hefty dose of I-don't-give-a-shit-anymore. And she'd only had a few sips—just enough to take the edge off and soften her mood.

She lifted her chin. "Did you know I got shot?"

Cole's head tipped to the side. His palm rested on her knee, threatening to rob coherent thought away as his body heat pressed into her flesh. Gently, his fingers squeezed her thigh in a move that was equal parts protective and sensual. Rylan was glad she didn't have to choose between the two; she loved them both.

"Ah, no."

Rylan tossed back her hair. His expression darkened as she slid the silk skirt up her until her left leg was bare to where her thigh creased against her thong. She pointed to a small pucker mark on her skin about three inches down from her hip.

"I took down a rapist and got a bullet right there. Chased him through a bar and the bastard shot me. I still took him down, bleeding all over the place." She nodded. "That made me a hero, apparently. Was just doing my job. I caught the judge's eye and stupid me thought I actually meant something to him."

Cole turned his body to fully face her, his grip on her leg pressing firmer. His lashes flickered. A small muscle jerked in his cheek, and if she didn't know better—because, really, Cole Haywood could not be capable of having real emotion on her behalf, not as hot and cold as he'd been toward her— he looked intensely angry.

"What happened?" He brushed the back of her upper arm with the fingers of his free hand. A liquid hot shiver went through her as she let the skirt fall.

"I was a cover." She fiddled with an earring, knowing that she should really, really stop talking, but she couldn't seem to. "That's why he wouldn't touch me, you know, more than once every few months. I was just the cover-up for his dirty little secret. I was the safe wife—the face for the media to latch onto for his up-and-coming political campaign." She leaned closer, wishing she'd had a little more wine before she quickly realized she didn't really need it. For some morbid reason, spilling her guts to Cole felt kind of nice. "I didn't take his name when we married. *That* really pissed him off."

He took a slow breath, his eyebrows hitching for her to continue. "A cover?"

God, how she wanted to lean into him. Feel those strong arms around her. Part the unbuttoned opening of his shirt and taste the tan skin over his collarbone. Fantasy. Pure, wonderful, delicious fantasy.

Too bad her real life had been anything but. "The second time I ever drank wine was the day I found the judge… fucking a hooker on my kitchen table."

Cole's balance slipped against the bar. Rylan's eyes went huge when she saw his reaction, but how could he help it? These things were just spilling out of her mouth, as calm and easy as if this were an everyday conversation about the weather or what to have for dinner. He suspected she hadn't even had much to drink. She was too steady, her voice too even. The little bit she'd had probably helped loosen her reserve, but the rest was her own doing. Why the hell did she want him to know these things, and worse, why did he feel so invested?

The soft give of her thigh under his hand reminded him he was crossing a line…again. He was touching her, again. And he couldn't give a flying fuck. He wanted Rylan to keep talking, to let him in on her secrets. It pained him to know the hurt look in her eyes—rimmed with real, vivid agony— was caused by a man who was supposed to love her. He couldn't stop the memory of how she'd cared for Birdie this morning—how deeply the tender side of her got under his skin. He couldn't shake it off. All day, he'd been trying, but the warm flush pumping through his veins wouldn't go away. Now, he didn't want it to.

Her eyes took on a far-off glow. "It didn't take me long to find out he had a fetish for prostitutes and vodka. Who in the hell could trust a drunk judge with a taste for whores, right? Enter me, the perfect wife. The perfect cover for his vices. Wine didn't take the stab of that realization away. Getting shot felt better."

Crickets roared in Cole's ears as he righted himself with a hand on the bar, the usual soft timbre of the night suddenly a blaring symphony. Adrenaline pumped through him, jacking his testosterone and fueling him with the urge to rip the judge apart. What a piece of shit. Stunned didn't quite fit what was tearing through him. Cole let the emotions steer him until he stood before her.

Enough of fighting it. He wanted a taste—no, he wanted to show Rylan that she was so much more than a sick man's pawn. Her eyes flashed silver as he placed both palms on her knees. The silk of her dress was like heaven's own clouds under his hands. It glided easily, lusciously over her legs, and he ran his hands slowly up her thighs. Rylan caught her breath, one hand coming to rest on his shoulder. She dug her fingers in—to hang on, he realized with a swell of ego, not push him away.

Vanilla notes wafted around him as he brought his face inches from hers. Her lips were parted and so tempting. Denying himself and diverting the encouragement in her expression, Cole leaned in next to her ear. Glossy strands of her hair tickled his mouth and chin. Cole let out a wedged breath and inhaled deeply the smooth scent of woman and blackberry wine. He didn't know what paralyzed him more, the info dump she'd just let loose or his cock throbbing urgently from her softness in his arms.

She held her breath for a beat, and it thrilled him. Her free hand found its mark on his other shoulder as his hands moved just a little higher. Cole glanced down at the tight contours of her tender thighs, half bared to him. Just a little higher and he'd see that satiny white string of her thong that she'd flashed him earlier. Just a little more and he'd lose it completely, press his mouth to the inside of her beautiful thigh and work his way up—

Rylan's fingers followed his shoulders to the curve of his neck, up until the bare skin heated under her tender caress.

Her fingers found his hair. "Are you coming on to me, Mr. Haywood?"

He bristled a little at the title but shoved it aside as hard as he could. There wouldn't be any "Mr. Haywood" bullshit. Not right now. His lips dipped behind her left ear. He let a little stream of breath wash over her flesh, making her tremble, before he pressed his mouth to her skin.

"That would be deliciously, wickedly inappropriate, don't you think?" He nuzzled the soft column of her throat, his hands going another inch higher toward her hips.

"Oh, yes." Her breathy words were more of a moan. Tonight, he wasn't her boss. He never wanted to be her boss again—hell, *he'd* quit if it meant one no-strings night with Rylan, to be her lover and get it out of his system. A tremor went through him at the promise of that, a deep realization flagging him.

"Say my name." She'd never said it, and he couldn't go another moment without hearing it. Cole licked the sensitive skin just below her ear before capturing her lobe between his lips as his fingers squeezed her thighs. She jumped a little before sinking into his touch.

Her smoky voice shook. "Mr. Haywood."

"Is that how you really think of me?" Cole held back a growl at the formality, his fingers digging a little harder into the delectable flesh of her thighs. He nipped her ear just enough to make her gasp. Rylan turned her head and broke free, her hands palming his cheeks and positioning his mouth in line with hers. Their breath mingled, hot and sweet.

"That's how I *should* think of you."

His fingers slid under the bunched skirt, over bare flesh to grip the bones of her hips. Her legs quivered, her eyes going heavy with desire.

"But is it?"

Without hesitation, she shook her head. Cole brought his lips to hers, tasted her with a quick slide of his lips from one corner of her mouth to the other. She shuddered, leaned in just as he pulled away.

"Say it. I want to hear your sexy voice say my name."

Her eyelids fell halfway, her lips parted just enough to show him the small tip of her tongue as she wet them.

"Cole."

Fucking. Christ. His cock squeezed and throbbed with fury. Cole nudged her legs wide with his hip and settled between her thighs as he pulled her hips down to his pelvis. Her bottom slid to the edge of the stool, her center joining him in a soft, hot caress against every inch of his aching, demanding erection. Her hands assumed a vise grip on his face, her lips grinding against his with a fire he needed more of. Wanted more of. Right damn now.

"Say it again," he demanded. She slanted her head to take his mouth fully, the dance of her tongue creating amazing friction against his. God, his head was swimming, and it was so, so good.

"Cole." The gravel in her voice nailed him. "I'll say it all night if you want me to." She pulled back with a heavy pant. He stiffened a moment at her words, his blood near boiling in the best way possible. But then her thighs clenched around his hips, drawing her soft center against him harder. One hand wandered to his back, pulling him against her breasts and holding him tight. Save for the narrow edge of stool still under her butt, she was clinging to him, and it was nowhere near close enough.

He wanted her in his bed. Under him. Screaming his name. Fuck the consequences. He'd been dying to worship her body from the day he'd walked her to the stables. Knowing what she'd been through with a shithole husband, now he wanted it that much more. Cole brought his mouth back to hers and was just about to swallow her moan when a voice cleared behind him. Needles raced over his back, his head whipping to the side. A security guard shone his light on them, a grim look on his bearded face.

"Party's over, you two. Take it inside."

"You've got to be kidding me," Cole grumbled, turning back to Rylan and tipping his forehead to her chest. A small, disbelieving laugh bubbled up and escaped her mouth. Cole smiled in response.

"Yes, sir," he called out without looking.

Rylan scooted backward onto the stool. Cole reluctantly supported her, missing the heat and sensual feel of her body as she regained her original position on the seat. The security guard cleared his throat again, obviously not happy that they weren't moving on immediately. Cole considered barking that he was the owner of the damn place, but one look at Rylan's expression told him the mood was cooling. Disappointment enveloped him at the uncertainty in her eyes—as if she were quietly examining what had just passed between them and second-guessed it all.

He wasn't second-guessing a goddamn thing. He still wanted her, against his better judgment, against history as a past indicator of future success. As he took Rylan's hand, helped her down, and led her from the tent, he had the nagging suspicion he'd always want her—no matter how many times he might bury himself in her body. They strolled under a brilliant moon toward the ranch house, his cock and her breathing having a hard time getting the message that sexy-times had been aborted for the moment.

He turned to her at the base of the steps and pulled her in against his chest. To his relief, Rylan's arms went up and around his neck without hesitation. Her nipples pebbled against him hard enough that he could feel it through the layers of clothing between them. Ice and fire decided to breed painful babies in his balls. Cole tugged on her hair, just enough to tip her head back. It wouldn't take much to rekindle the fire. He gritted his teeth. When it happened between them, he didn't want either of them to regret a single moment. The uncertainty behind the passion in her eyes told him this wasn't that moment.

"You're going to go in the house, slip into your room, and lock the door behind you. Understand?" He tracked the movement of her throat as she swallowed. "If you don't, we're going to finish what we started, and you'll scream my name until you're hoarse."

She paused, then pulled her lower lip between her teeth right before she gave a reluctant nod. Rylan reached up on tiptoe to kiss him softly, her fingers streaking over his face.

"Good night, Cole." She turned and ascended the porch stairs. Her footfalls padded across the wood, the *click* and *clack* of the door swallowing her. Cole looked up at the bright stars as he fought with his body to cool the fuck down. He ached for her, in more ways than one. Sex, yes. But his arms ached too, just to hold her, to pull her body tightly next to him as she slept and inhale the sweet scent of her hair. Good night? Nope. There would be nothing good about the hours that separated him from the dawn. Not one thing.

Chapter Ten

Wine. Yeah, that was a really bad idea. Rylan unloaded the dishwasher with a throb drumming in her head. It matched the nagging ache between her legs that had refused to go away since last night. Damn Cole and his naughty, incredible mouth. She paused to take in the pasture view outside the kitchen window, a dinner plate in each hand. The view was so amazing—lush green highlighted with foggy mountains in the backdrop—she lost her thoughts for a moment.

But then memories of the night before came back hard and insistent. She had made a fool of herself, her tongue especially when it wagged her sob story. Cole had looked so good, his light-blue shirt halfway unbuttoned and untucked from his jeans. Her mouth had needed something to do, and since she'd known better than to drink anymore, it was either talk or lick him from here to there. Talking seemed safer, but she'd pretty much ended up licking him anyway. What the hell was wrong with her?

Cole Haywood was off-limits. She knew it, but she didn't feel it. He was her boss, and more importantly, a single father. He and Birdie were a matched set, and no matter how much she might want Cole, she wasn't emotionally ready to take on a child. Not in a capacity more than their current situation required. Boots scuffing the floor grabbed her attention, and she turned. Cole nodded in greeting and set a coffee cup on the counter, a slow grin pulling at his lips as if he knew she'd just been thinking about him.

Her chest did a little flippy thing at the sight of him. Untucked gray T-shirt, no hat, wet hair, beat-up old Wranglers, and boots. Jesus, the man could wear a tarp and drop a woman dead. Blood rushed in her ears, and her shoulders tensed a little. Last night... *Oh, man.*

"You know, that isn't going to work around here." The sound of his voice, all gravelly and male, made Rylan close her eyes a moment just to experience it. It wasn't only the sound of his voice—it was the feeling that washed over her when she heard it. He winked and waved a finger at her feet, the gesture bringing a smile to her lips. Rylan glanced down. Her ripped Silver jeans were rolled calf-high, and her gray Wisconsin Badgers T-shirt was a little faded. After the beautiful dress she'd worn yesterday, she was sure she looked like a hungover hillbilly.

"Umm, what?"

"Those." Cole hitched one leg and pointed at her feet. "Whatever those are."

Rylan stuck a foot out and wiggled her toes with a flush of heat over her chest. Last night should have hung like an elephant over them, but his easy demeanor and the teasing twinkle in his eyes was putting her at ease.

"This nifty invention is called a sandal. A Birkenstock, to be exact."

"Yeah, well, sandals aren't going to cut it." He leaned his ass against the counter, his eyes unabashedly drinking her in. Rylan made a mocking sound.

"Ah yes. I forgot that I need skintight Wranglers, a sparkly shirt, and some kick-ass boots to mop the floor and do the laundry." She braced her hands on the counter behind her and tilted back. A brilliant smile cut across his rugged face, flashing her those perfect, white teeth. The slight upturn of his upper lip was more pronounced, making his mouth all the more appealing.

"You have a sexy smile." Rylan hitched a half breath, her cheeks growing ice-cold. The breath came back out in a rush as she looked down and crossed her ankles with a little laugh. "Ah, yeah, that wasn't supposed to actually come out of my mouth."

Cole chuckled, the response surprising her. She dared look at him, her scalp tingling to see a swipe of pink across his cheeks. It must be the light, because men like Cole did not blush at a tiny compliment. She shook her head and turned back to the dishes. He needed to get out of the kitchen before she said more stupid things, like how much she'd loved what happened between them last night, how much she wanted more.

"Okay, get out of here. You're in my way."

"Look at me, Rylan." The command wasn't gentle, and the hairs on the back of her neck stood up, her pulse notching again. She turned to meet his gaze for a fraction of a second before looking away.

"Nope. Right here." He pointed to his eyes and she

followed, lost in the bright glow of his expression with its underlying smolder. "Thank you," he said. "For the compliment." He wasn't smiling anymore.

She cleared her throat. "Yeah. You're welcome." She turned back to her work before something else ridiculous spouted out of her.

"By the way, you have an incredible ass." Cole clomped out of the kitchen as Rylan's head snapped up. "And if you have something besides *Birkenstocks* to wear, meet me at the barn in half an hour. You can ride out to the west pastures with me."

Hell, she'd find something else to wear if it killed her.

• • •

The squeak of the saddle was a familiar, comforting sound as Rylan rode alongside Cole, drinking in the scenery as they walked their horses across the plain. Everything seemed to be in full bloom—purple and pink flowers dotting the grassy land, the evergreens bright and vibrant shades of green, the mountains subdued in azure and gray. A wide-open stretch of grassland lined by a lush pine ridge bordering the base of the mountain stretched out before them. Back home in Wisconsin, she'd been raised on 140 acres of hay field. Not a mountain or hill in sight.

As beautiful as the scenery was, though, it did little to take her mind off Cole or the fact that he'd barely said two words since they left the barn. The silence was fine by her. It gave her the chance to rope her nerves into submission and settle the slight awkwardness that they hadn't addressed their near-miss late-night romp.

Cole's brown-and-white overo was taller than hers, and Rylan had to admit Cole was an impressive sight on top of that powerful horse. "It's beautiful out here, isn't it?"

She knew he'd been watching her as she took it all in. The heat on her cheeks wasn't just from the sun. "Yeah. It's amazing."

He took off his hat and ran fingers through his hair before setting it back on. "It's easy to take this place for granted. Sometimes, I just forget to look anymore." The slight longing in his tone took her off guard and raised a protective feeling. He was so damn busy all the time she didn't doubt for one second that slower moments like this didn't happen nearly as often as they should.

Rylan's horse sidestepped, driving her knee into Cole's leg. "Sorry." She was still getting used to the sturdy gelding beneath her. Exceptionally trained, he was cued in to leg pressure that Rylan wasn't completely familiar with. One unintentional movement of her legs had the poor horse going in all sorts of directions. Though she'd grown up riding, her all-around quarter horse wasn't trained quite as impressively as the one she was on right now.

She opened her mouth to say something about last night, realized she hadn't really thought about *what* to say, cleared her throat, and changed her mind.

"Dad milked eighty-five head of Holstein," she said. "There wasn't much to see beyond the cows and the corn. Not like here at all."

"Huh." Cole let his forearms rest on the pommel. "I didn't figure you for a farm girl."

"How did you figure me, exactly?" Rylan asked, as she heard the trickle of water ahead. She searched the land for the source.

Cole shrugged. "I don't know. I figured any woman who grows up to be a city cop probably had it rough as a kid."

Rylan laughed, turning to him. "Well, getting up to milk cows at four-thirty a.m. before school every day *was* rough, thank you. That and smelling slightly like cow shit all the time." Her horse bumped Cole's again, their legs hitting hard this time.

Cole reached out and gave her horse a shove on the neck. "Loosen your right leg. Just let it fall. Put pressure on his side with your left calf, like you're trying to push him over your leg." Rylan did what he suggested, and the horse took three wide steps to the right.

The slight distance between her and Cole gave her a fresh dose of bravery. Whatever was going on between them needed to be voiced. She couldn't go another night replaying it all in her mind, wondering what he really wanted from her and pondering just how much she was able to give. It was maddening.

"Cole, uh, about—"

"Any siblings work the farm with your dad?" The easy smile had slipped from his lips. Rylan rolled her eyes, figuring his time-to-come-clean sensor went off and prompted him to hedge.

"My dad is still on the farm, but the cows are long gone. He rents out the land now. I only have one brother, Robert, in Australia. He and his partner, Trey, are expecting a baby via surrogate anytime."

He gave a little nod, his only response.

They cleared a small hill, and the glint of water came into view. A river snaked across the grassland, disappearing to the east while the mountain to the north swallowed it up.

"Come on." Cole urged his horse to a trot. Rylan followed suit, going down the hill toward the water. Her breath caught when she spied the riverbank. Multicolored stones stretched along the banks just below the shallow surface. A palette of dusky red and pink, purple, blue, and green rocks twinkled in the sun. Cole reined up next to her, a half smile on his face. He looked pleased by her awe.

"Welcome to Paint River," he said. Rylan followed him in a dismount. Cole knelt beside the river and splayed his hand over the surface. "Looks like someone painted rocks and threw them out there, huh?"

The colorful stones lay on the muddy banks and inched a few feet into the river, disappearing into the depths. Cole picked up a few stones and set them in his palm. They were smooth and flat, their colors faded somewhat once removed from the water. "This is the only river to have colored stones in this abundance. Been here for as long as anyone can remember."

Rylan trailed her fingers over the stones, gracing Cole's skin as she did. She realized he'd tracked the movements of her fingers, then watched her as she picked one up and turned it side to side. He dumped the rocks back in and stood, putting a hand on her shoulder.

"See that?" Cole indicated with his head toward an oak tree spread out among a small grouping of trees near a curve in the river. It had a twisted trunk and branches that arched and spread like arms stretched wide. Cole walked toward the tree, beckoning Rylan along. He dropped his horse's reins and disappeared under the canopy. Curious, Rylan did the same. Inside, the tree made an umbrella of beautifully curved branches just high enough that they could walk under them.

She looked up, surprise making her momentarily speechless. Objects hung from the oak's low branches. Strands of faded ribbon, a silver spoon, a tiny baby shoe. The little treasures hung down like a weathered, eccentric wind chime. There could easily be hundreds of small tidbits hanging from the tree.

Rylan traced the baby shoe with a fingertip. It was easily early 1900s, with cracking black leather and tiny pearl side buttons. She gave a disbelieving laugh. "What is this?"

Cole braced one hand on the tree trunk. "That would be a shoe."

Rylan whipped him an amused smile. "This." She swept her arms wide, nodding to the tree. Cole smiled teasingly and flicked a gray wooden pipe hanging from a strip of leather.

"It's the Wishing Tree. Legend has it that you leave the tree a gift, and it grants you a wish." His shoulder brushed her arm.

Rylan moved farther away, looking at the items in the branches. "Got anything to wish for, Cole?"

Cole smirked. "Nope. I don't believe in shit like this. No sense in making wishes. If I want something, I grab it myself."

Images of last night uncoiled in her mind. Yes, he certainly did.

"Some things aren't tangible, though," she said. "There are some things the universe takes care of for you." She moved around the tree's circumference, taken aback at the antiquity of some of the trinkets. Silverware, a small brass hairbrush with horsehair bristles, a gold wedding band. Rylan pulled the branch down to peer at the ring more closely.

Inside, an engraving read "Cherished Wife." The sheer magnitude of how many people must have crossed this land in the past became an exciting reality as she looked at what they'd left behind.

"That's silly," Cole replied. He was right behind her, his body heat rolling over her neck.

"Living intentionally isn't dumb. If you want the universe to help you with something, you have to ask for it. You have to put it out there, make it known." She looked over her shoulder. Cole's face was doubtful. "Everyone who put something here believed in the power of making a wish."

"How many do you think actually came true, Rylan?"

Her lower lip jutted out. "I don't know. But I don't think it hurts to try. Sometimes you just need help to get the things you want the most."

She turned to face him at the same time he stepped closer. Dark hair spilled from beneath his hat when he cocked his head. His eyes found her lips, his own parting just a bit.

"What do you want the most, Rylan?"

"Mmm, personal question." Shaking inside, Rylan gave a teasing frown. "I could ask you the same but I doubt I'd get an honest answer."

Cole stepped in again, all humor gone from his face. The sudden intensity made her breasts ache. She retreated a step, her rear bumping into the tree, her palms down on the rough surface. Cole braced one hand over her shoulder on the trunk and leaned in close. Rylan's lips tingled with his proximity.

"Are you sure you really want to know?" His chest rose and fell behind the snug gray cotton. Excitement and longing flooded her veins.

"Yes."

His put his other hand against the tree, completely boxing her in. "What I want the most right damn now it to forget, for *one day*, that I'm your boss so I can make love to you with no regrets and no what-ifs." Rylan's breath left in a *whoosh*. She looped her hands around his hard biceps to keep steady as her legs suddenly felt unable to keep her standing. She knew he wanted her, but hearing him voice the confession drove it home.

"I know we shouldn't…but I want that, too. So much." And they shouldn't, they really shouldn't. At least, she shouldn't if she knew what was smart for her heart, the healing process, and her job. But no matter how she tried to rationalize all the reasons not to fall into Cole's arms, the harder it got to justify why she shouldn't. The lines got all blurry while her body simply ached for him more. Maybe it was a sign that she needed to stop overthinking and just let life happen.

God, would her therapist be proud of her.

Cole ran a hand over her cheek, his fingers lifting her chin for a gentle kiss. "You're right. We shouldn't. But I'm beyond caring about that right now." He pushed away from the tree, leaving her bereft and empty. She hated that she felt so damn needy—that she couldn't seem to shove that need far, far away like she did everything else. Coming to the ranch had loosened her ability to restrain her emotions, and she wasn't sure how to handle this new *feely* Rylan.

Cole reached for her hand. She took it as he pulled her into an embrace. Desire flushed to the surface of her skin, jacking her heart rate again.

"You really need to stop doing this to me," she uttered.

"My heart is going to give out."

He nuzzled her neck. "If you think the reasons we should are stronger than the reasons we shouldn't, keep your bedroom door unlocked tonight." *Flip, flip, crash*. Her poor, poor heart. *Let life—and great sex—happen*. Great sex, with her boss.

Her brow fell. He'd probably change his mind. And if he did, it would be *fine*. She wasn't looking for a relationship—the possibility of intimacy with Cole was just a bonus. But if he did change his mind, this heat between them was going to boil over until one of them, maybe both, exploded from the buildup. If he didn't, they could let it buck and see what happened. He wouldn't want more than sex, and neither did she. And if he could push past the fact that he was her boss, then it wouldn't matter to her either. They'd keep it quiet—go about their normal routine with no reason for anything to be different.

Nothing had to change. She didn't have to get invested in his personal life, just worship his body.

Rylan fingered a lock of hair away from his brow. "It'll be open." A gravelly moan came from deep in his throat as he bent down to kiss her. At the same time, his cell phone went nuts. He hesitated before finally pulling away with a curse, his fingers taking their time sliding away from her back.

He read a message. "The vet's here. I need to get back." Rylan followed him out from under the tree to where their horses grazed. She mounted, Cole doing the same.

They cantered up and over the hill, leaving the rush of the river behind. Rylan reined up next to him as they slowed to a walk.

"I wanted to tell you... About the things I said last

night…" She paused, and he looked over at her. "I'm sorry I spilled my sob story on you."

Cole's hand snaked out to grab her wrist, his fingers giving her a tender squeeze.

"Don't be." A slow grin hitched one corner of his mouth. The five-o'clock shadow on his angular jaw begged her to reach out and touch it. The blue of his eyes dared her to get lost. "Two things, Rylan. One: you're an amazing woman with more backbone than half the men I know. Two: the judge was so unworthy of you. It pisses me off to think you wasted one tear on him. Understand?"

A sudden burst of emotion from his praise caused a lump in her throat. She could only nod, smiling like an idiot as they urged the horses into a run toward the ranch.

Chapter Eleven

Handbook, handbook, handbook. He was going to burn them. Every single one. One hand on her doorknob, his heart pounding, his brain trying to rationalize common sense and failing, Cole turned the knob.

Unlocked.

Just as she'd said it would be. Anticipation flooded him as he pushed the door open and entered Rylan's room. He'd pull off his plan and they'd talk, lay some ground rules. Decide what would happen between them and what wouldn't. If the lines were crystal clear, his heart, his ranch, and his daughter wouldn't be at risk.

Cole ran his hand along the curve of Rylan's waist as she lay in bed. Her body was sleep-warmed and tantalizing under his palm. Sliding in next to her was so damn tempting, but he had different plans. He didn't want to risk interruption and wanted Rylan to be comfortable enough to enjoy every second of what he had in mind. She'd never let loose under this roof.

She moaned and shifted as he slipped the quilt off her body. Cole lifted her easily, and her head lolled against his shoulder. She sighed as her eyes fluttered open. He whipped a small blanket over her and strode to the door. She tried to sit in his arms, her hands grabbing his shoulders as though she might fall.

"Just be still." He kissed Rylan's temple as she came fully awake.

"What the hell is this?" Her breathy voice made his heart leap.

"Me kidnapping you."

He followed the hall around the kitchen to the back door. Outside, the warm summer breeze rippled the ends of her hair across his face. She tried again to sit up, gasping when she saw his horse waiting by the back porch. Flickers of surprise and joy and want crossed her face, and to his relief, not a single sign of hesitation. Still, he had to be sure. His lips found the hair just above her ear.

"You can tell me to stop right now." *Tell me to stop before I lose myself in you.*

"Don't stop."

Cole set her in the saddle and swung up behind her. His hand found her chin to turn her his way for a soft kiss before his arms banded around her, and he kicked the horse into a canter. Her hips rocked back against his groin as her body softened against his. Perfection. He couldn't wait for more.

Moonlight beamed a silver path through the darkness, and Cole's horse went easily across the flat and over the hills. The war in his head over the sanity of letting this happen between them made peace with itself, leaving him to enjoy having her in his arms, her head against his chest. Her face lifted at the first sparkle of golden light. She sat a little straighter, her hands looped around his neck as the luxury tents came into view. He'd come out here earlier and prepared the farthest tent on the left. Strands of light over the front peak were lit, the door flap open so the kerosene lamps inside cast flickering light into the night.

Rylan's excited intake of breath made sneaking up here totally worth it.

"Surprised?" He palmed hair away from her forehead and ran his fingers down the silky strands.

"Yes." Rylan shivered. He ran his hands over the bare length of her arms before jumping down to open the gate. He led the horse through, latched the gate again, and willed his heart to slow down as the horse followed him to the tent. His gut was in knots when he reached for her, pulled her down into his arms, and kissed her. Her hands clenched on his shoulders as he took her mouth hard and deep. Waiting was no longer an option.

Rylan pulled back. "Take me inside." When her fingers fumbled with the top button on his shirt, Cole couldn't move fast enough. He carried her up the steps and inside, setting her down at the foot of the bed. Awash in the soft light, Rylan was sexier than any woman he'd ever seen or could have imagined—nightshirt clinging to her curves, her hair messy and loose, lips swollen from his kiss. Even sexier was how she looked at him and didn't stop, not even to look around the tent he'd remembered she loved so much.

She was focused on him alone, and it inflamed him to near combustion.

He gently pushed her backward, their eyes connected

in a battle of passion and restraint. The sound of crickets and rustling leaves mixed with the sound of Rylan's heavy breathing. The music made his groin ache. He watched her lips, focused on the rise and fall of her chest to keep his passion under control.

He pushed her back another step until her ass pressed against the foot of the bed. His hand slid against her thigh as she moved back, glided up to the curve of her hip—the naked curve.

"No panties," he said with the arch of one brow. Rylan in bed, nightshirt hiked up to her belly, naked underneath—

She grabbed the back of his head with one hand, his fantasy coming to life in her words. "I was dreaming about you and they got in the way."

Jesus. Christ. His cock swelled as he pulled her against him. "Fuck."

"Yes, please." Her nipples pebbled against his chest, her head tipping back, leaving the column of her smooth throat open to his lips. Cole's mouth burned to taste her.

Not yet.

He whipped off his hat and threw it across the room. He lightly gripped her wrists, pressing her between the bed frame and his body. Her thighs were hot against his. Knowing she was naked under that shirt made him wish he could blink and make his own clothes disappear so he could be naked and tangled with her, long legs wrapped around him, pulling him in. *Soon.*

"What do you want from me?" Cole gripped her arms tighter. Her expression was sultry, lips slightly parted and eyes wide with a dark haze that turned them the color of campfire smoke. She didn't display a lick of inhibition—instead she radiated the pure sexuality of a woman who knew what she wanted.

"I want you to kiss me…everywhere." She squirmed. A thread of resolve snapped, and he dipped his head to place little kisses over her jaw. She inhaled a sharp breath, pressed her breasts up against him.

"No." He nibbled her ear. "What do you want besides this? Besides sex?" Hell, what did he want? When his mind was quiet and let him dream, he wanted the slide of her hand in his palm, the sound of her voice filling his home, the exquisite warmth of her body in his bed each night. Yet every time he awakened to the real desires of his heart, the betrayals of the past made the idea of ever falling in love again a dark, terrifying notion.

Rylan's lashes fluttered. "What do you mean?"

Cole licked the outer shell of her ear as her body stretched out beneath him. "What do you *want*, Rylan?" Leaning back, he appreciated the beautiful swell of her breasts with their hard, dark-rose nipples. Shit, the way they tasted on his tongue. His mouth trailed along her neck, stopping to trace her collarbone. His free hand caressed her ribs and the side of her breast through the shirt.

She shuddered hard. "Can't we just have this?"

Bingo.

It was all the cue he needed. He found the bottom of her shirt and pulled it up, smoothing the fabric up over her hips to her ribs, watching as each movement brought more of her incredible figure into his view. She didn't hesitate to raise her arms as he bared her breasts—holy shit, they were perfect—and pulled the shirt free from her body. Cole cupped her breasts and thumbed both taut nipples. She bucked hard against him. Damn, she was so ready. Cole wanted to replace his fingers with his lips, but he knew the minute that little pebble was in his mouth, he'd come undone.

"This is all I can offer you." Cole took her hand and led her around the bed, following her as she lay back, putting one knee between her thighs, and bracing himself on his arms. The inky darkness of her hair spread over the lace pillow, her golden skin shimmering in the candlelight.

"This is all *I* can offer you. Experiencing you is all I want." Her hands found the buttons on his shirt. His cock pulsed so hard he clenched his teeth against the pain.

His lips found her jaw. "I'm an experience?"

"Are you kidding me? Do you even look in the mirror?" Rylan tipped her chin, her luscious lips begging for his kiss. "You're gorgeous, strong, and sexy. The way you take care of Birdie, your dedication to your family and this ranch. What woman wouldn't want to experience you?" She leaned up, but Cole couldn't let her go. He traced her cheek with his fingers, the ache in his chest unfamiliar and excruciating. It didn't just hurt—it clenched and milked the essence right out of him.

He needed to put himself back into place. "Just blowing off steam."

"Yes."

Rylan grabbed big handfuls of his hair and arched up for his kiss. His lips slammed into hers, taking possession of her mouth the same way he knew she could easily take his heart. She was kindhearted, caring, and real. He didn't want to be putty in her hands but he was. He completely was, and this "blowing off steam" bit might be harder to rein in than he'd thought.

Her body was all soft curves and heat-flushed skin under

his hands, the perfect fit against his palms. Rylan pulled him down so hard he had no choice but to comply. Cole sank into her, holding himself up with one hand while the other traced every inch of her he could reach. His tongue slid along hers, warm and wet, nipping the tip gently until she moaned and pulled him even closer. He wanted to feel her mouth on him. Streaks of heat stroked his ribs as she pulled up his shirt, her fingertips racing along his sides. He'd barely pulled the shirt off when her hands were on his jeans, working the button. Cole grasped her hands.

"Sweetheart, slow down," he drawled. "I want to take my time."

She shook her head, eyes wide and smoky silver. "No. I want you now."

Rylan stretched like a cat, her glorious body inviting and open. Cole slid out of his jeans, remembered to dig a condom from the back pocket before they fell to the floor. He knelt between her legs, relishing the tremor that went through her as his hands ran up the insides of her thighs.

"I'm going to make you wait," he teased. "And you're going to lie here and enjoy it."

"But—"

Cole kissed her long and hard. "One more word and I'll leave you naked and wanting."

She shivered. "Yeah, righ—"

"Naked. And. Wanting." Cole bent to her belly and swirled little circles there with his tongue. She squirmed, her hips shifting as he worked lower until his mouth rested right above her curls.

The night was quiet and wrapped them in the heady scent of pine and sage. It was perfection. She was perfection.

He was looking forward to wrapping her in his arms and holding her all night as much as he wanted this, right now. By the time the night found morning, he'd be so far gone from the exquisite feel of her body he'd need a map to get back.

Her curls were soft and tickled his fingers as he ran a hand between her legs. She arched, her fingers winding in his hair. He'd meant to torture and tease her, but he was gently parting her and dipping his tongue inside her intense heat before he could stop himself. Rylan cried out, holding his head tightly while her legs went wide. She was so wet and sweet and exactly what he'd imagined. Her clit was hard and swollen when he loved it with his tongue. Cole's hands moved from her hips to her breasts, teased her nipples in time with his tongue until she shook and raked her short fingernails over his scalp.

He loved her nub with flat, purposeful strokes, finding the pressure, the rhythm that made her tense and shiver. The sensual slide of her body beneath him inflamed the desire he'd been holding back since the first day he'd seen her drinking coffee on the porch in the morning sunlight. Cole ran his hands down the length of her body, cupping the backs of her thighs. He brought her legs farther apart as his tongue stroked hard down her center. His name flew from her lips in a deep, shuddering sigh.

"Cole!"

God, he loved how she said his name. Her hands pressed against his temples as she urged him up. Cole tilted a glance at her, a wicked need pounding in his chest. Her face was flushed, her eyes heavy and lost, and it drove home every moment he'd waited to have her this way. He pushed up on his arms and grazed his body over hers, his length sliding along her center. Rylan's hands stroked his chest, his shoulders, her fingers drawing sparks everywhere she touched.

A flutter trailed over his middle as her fingers traced his skin right before her palm went flat and smoothed down, until she held him in one fast, hard grip. Cole jerked as she made an appreciative sound low in her throat. Rylan's hand began to stroke him with torturous, slow movements.

She made little circles with her thumb over his tip. Cole put his head to her chest, his back arched to press his hips deeper against her hand.

"Now, please. Now."

Her plea broke him. Cole flipped her onto her belly, one arm supporting her middle as he drew her onto her knees. His right hand moved between her legs, finding the pressure and rhythm that had sent her into a spiral before while he ripped open the condom packet with his free hand and teeth. Rylan looked at him over her shoulder, backed up against him with a moan, lowering her upper body. The invitation pushed him over the last edge of restraint. Her silky hair spread around her shoulders, the rusty red highlights flickering in the candlelight as he grabbed a handful and slid inside her. She pressed back against him, her sex tensing and quivering around him, urging him faster. Within her fully, Cole dipped his forehead to her back, forcing his hips to hold so he could absorb every electric shock rocketing through him.

Rylan's moans of urgency turned to fast, seductive pants as he worked her clit with his fingers. Her soft flesh heated under his touch, grew wetter as she shuddered violently.

"Please!" The word dripped off her moans. Cole pulled back, clenching his eyes at the sensation of his cock moving through the velvet of her soft heat. Teasing her, loving the tension rolling off her tight muscles and flushed skin, Cole held his tip precariously close to leaving her completely. She uttered something that sounded a lot like begging. Her need thrilled him, tortured him, and he fucking loved it.

He thrust into her in one easy motion, and Rylan shattered.

"Goddammit!" Cole bit his lip as the quake of Rylan's orgasm rippled around his cock. He rode her through it in even, deep strokes. Erotic sounds filled his head, the sound of their bodies coming together, her fingers dragging across the bed, their moans blending into one. Cole grabbed big handfuls of her hair, pulling her head back gently as the pressure in his groin built, his thighs growing tight until his climax couldn't be contained another second. He let himself go, pouring out in long, hard pulses. Rylan's entire body shuddered, and she went boneless beneath him. Cole wrapped his arms around her hips, holding them together until the lightning in his brain faded.

Rylan's skin was damp with sweat against him as he curled around her and lowered her to the sheets. She spooned into him with a breathy sigh. Cole listened to her breathing and the soft satiated moan that fell from her lips. The far-off cry of a coyote echoed in his ears. She turned in his arms, one hand resting against his jaw. Cole searched her eyes, wishing for just a moment that he'd see something in her eyes that told him she wanted to be more—that she could be the one for him. She smiled sleepily, her eyes closing as she rested her head beneath his chin.

Cole gathered her up and snuggled her close, his heart equally full and empty. He was already vulnerable, a place he hated to be.

"That was wonderful," she whispered, her left arm tightening around him as she wiggled even closer against him.

Wonderful? It rocked him completely off-center. Cole threaded his fingers through her hair and took a big breath of her sweet scent. "Amazing."

"I'm going to like blowing off steam with you," she said, her left leg smoothing over the top of his thigh. A small heaviness plunked through the middle of his sated fog. *Blowing off steam. Absolutely. That's all it could be.*

"Oh, sweetheart, me too."

Her narrow fingers traced a lazy path over his biceps as time ticked down. The coyotes sang, getting farther away until their sounds were replaced by an owl hooting near the tent. Rylan's even breathing told him she was close to sleep, if she wasn't already out. Reluctantly, he pulled back and gave her a gentle shake. He could stay here all night, but getting caught breaking his own rule wouldn't look too good. The sun would be up soon and so would the ranch hands. If he was going to get her back unseen, they needed to go now.

"We have to get back, Rylan."

She moaned and turned onto her back, pulling him with her. Cole's body jumped to life as her breasts pressed into his chest.

"Do we have time for one more round?"

Cole chuckled, moving reluctantly away before he was tempted to say yes. He handed Rylan her shirt while he stood to dress and paused to watch her slip the shirt over her head, each flutter of the fabric covering her body and filling him with disappointment. His blood still hummed, his skin alive with her touch. As he led her to the horse, he knew that one more time wouldn't be enough. A million times wouldn't be enough.

Chapter Twelve

The sweet ache between her legs made it hard for Rylan to keep a ridiculous grin off her face the next morning. When Tucker approached her about taking Maeve into Missoula for her doctor's appointments, Rylan happily agreed. She was riding an endorphin high and nothing was going to dampen it—not even knowing she'd have to watch Birdie while Maeve was in the clinic.

Missoula had all the amenities of a large city, most specifically, a Starbucks. The promise of an espresso-induced mouth orgasm was too good to pass up. The minute the coffee hit Rylan's lips, she knew she'd be flying all day. Good. It was about damn time. Maeve's appointments and testing would take a couple hours, too long for Birdie to sit and wait. Following Maeve's directions to the mall, Rylan figured she'd find a way to keep Birdie busy until Maeve was done.

Rylan had a soft spot for the child, she had to admit. Taking care of Birdie's injury the other day had touched her deeply. It felt good to be needed that way, and Birdie seemed happy to continue stomping on Rylan's emotions by bouncing around in a tutu, curls flying, big blue eyes sparkling like rain. And then her heart would break all over again. Any other child? Well, other kids went home. Not Birdie. She lived under the same roof, subjecting Rylan to her girlish giggles and the patter of her fat little feet every single day. It was slow torture seeing, hearing, touching this child who reminded her so much of Rachel. Yet as the days passed, it started to feel less and less uncomfortable and more tolerable. Nice, even.

Rylan wasn't sure what Birdie was more excited about, going to the mall now or her upcoming fifth birthday party. She nearly pulled Rylan's pinky finger off with her strong little grip as she beelined for the ice cream kiosk, eagerly jumping into a ridiculously long line. As they waited, Birdie chattered nonstop about birthday cake and presents, her hand settling completely into Rylan's. Memories of holding Rachel's hand when she'd just learned to walk rubbed their way to the surface. The closer they got to their turn to order, the harder Birdie squeezed her hand. It didn't take long for the little girl's excitement to become contagious.

They sat at a bench after getting their treats. Birdie watched drips roll off her cone, rushing to catch a few with her tongue. "Uncle Levi has that," Birdie said in between drip-chasing. Rylan followed her gaze across the hall to a store selling ready-to-stuff teddy bears.

"What does Levi have?"

Birdie pointed to the poster on one of the store windows that showed a bear with an American flag stitched on its chest, wearing military camouflage pants and a cap. Rylan lowered her cone. As far as she understood, Birdie had never met her uncle Levi. He'd left for the military before she'd been born and hadn't been home since. That she recalled enough about him from what her family had told her was sweet and heartbreaking all at once.

"Levi wears those same clothes?"

Birdie nodded in agreement.

A thought popped into Rylan's head. "Should we make one of those bears for Levi? You could send it to him in a care package, like when Grandma sends him things."

Birdie jumped up from the bench, took a huge bite off the top of her cone, and threw the rest in the trash. *I guess that's a yes.* Rylan laughed and grabbed Birdie's sticky hand.

"Let's go wash up first." They headed through the crowded mall to the bathroom. On the way, Rylan noticed a well-dressed woman in a hot-pink sundress across the hall. Her glittery blond hair was smoothed in a perfect ponytail, golden necklaces and bangles completing the polish that made her stand out among the jeans-and-T-shirt-clad crowd. Rylan felt a moment of envy. Didn't every woman want to look like that just once?

On their way back to the teddy bear store, Birdie pulled Rylan into a toy store and filled her arms with baby dolls. Then off to a clothing boutique where she fingered sunglasses and floppy hats and sparkly sandals. Rylan smiled when Birdie modeled for her, feeling an inkling of lightness creep through her inner walls at the sound of Birdie's laughter. Unlike most kids on shopping trips, Birdie didn't ask for anything. She perused the goods with joy and put them back when she was done. They made a teddy bear for Levi, complete with camo pants, a jacket, and cap they had embroidered with his name. By the time they were done, more than two hours had passed and Rylan had barely noticed.

"It's time to pick up Grandma and get back to Paint River, Birdie. Are you ready?" Rylan helped Birdie put the bear in a bag. They stepped out of the store, nearly colliding with the woman in pink by the exit. Rylan stopped short to avoid running into her, pulling Birdie back with her.

Rylan gasped. "I'm sorry. We didn't see you."

The woman had a collected smile and her light-blue eyes clung to Birdie with a ferocity that Rylan found a little alarming. Maybe it was her cop Spidey-sense going off again, but the look had "opportune kidnapper" written all over it. Rylan strengthened her grip on Birdie's wrist.

"Excuse me," the woman said, crossing her hands in front of her. "I couldn't help overhearing that you're going to Paint River Ranch?"

Rylan nodded. "Yes."

"Is Cole Haywood there?" she asked. "I just… He hasn't returned my calls, so I was wondering if he was home." An image of Cole's lips came to mind. How they'd tasted on hers. The feel of his body sliding in and out of hers.

"Um, yes, he's there," Rylan replied with tension squeezing her gut.

"Cole is my daddy!" Birdie's possessive voice came from behind Rylan's legs. The woman smiled and gave Birdie a little wave.

"I know, sweetie. I know your daddy *real* well." She turned back to Rylan, the cool smile gone. "And you are?"

Rylan tipped her chin up at the woman's haughty tone. Her endorphins were still running smooth and high. Fine, she'd play nice. She extended a hand. The woman didn't take it.

"I'm Rylan,"

"She's the housekeeper!" Birdie chimed in again, climbing both her hands up Rylan's forearm. Rylan grimaced. The woman cleared her throat with a small smile on her pouty lips.

Rylan stomped down the flicker of self-consciousness welling inside her. What the hell did it matter if this magazine Barbie knew that she was the housekeeper? "Shall I give Cole a message?"

The woman shook her head, an amused glint in her frosty eyes. "No." And she spun on one nude heel and left. Rylan riffled through the possibilities of who Barbie might be as the woman walked away. Cole's lover? Business associate? Family friend? Right, she was going with lover. Jealousy wanted to snake in, but Rylan refused. They had a no-commitment agreement, and Cole had been with *her* last night. No one else. That was all that mattered. Even as she tried to rationalize it, her brain growled out one word: *mine!*

Rylan refocused. Cole certainly wasn't hers, and she needed to stop reading into it right now, take what he could give, and enjoy the hell out of it. Rylan reached her hand to Birdie.

"Ready, Birdie?" The little girl grabbed on to Rylan's pinky and started swinging their connected hands.

"Can we go home and see my daddy?"

Rylan's chest flushed with warmth. That was the best idea they'd had all day.

• • •

The big house took on an unusual hush that night. Rylan was accustomed to the sound of Cole or Tucker coming and going, or Birdie's nightly fracas to put off going to sleep. Sitting on the middle of her bed, Rylan focused on her breathing and relished the quiet. Their long day in town had likely pooped Birdie right out. Rylan was certainly tired. She lay back on the mattress, recognizing how much she'd enjoyed spending time with Birdie today. Watching her eat ice cream, the way one finger made little trails in the drips over the waffle cone, tipped the whole thing off. After that, Rylan had found herself observing all the little nuances—facial expressions, the way she said certain words, how her tongue stuck out when she concentrated—that made Birdie, Birdie.

Rylan frowned a little and closed her eyes tighter. An image materialized in her mind's eye. A pair of huge brown eyes with long, curling lashes over almond-shaped eyes. A small rosebud mouth, hair the color of morning sun. The lips smiled and then the image was gone.

Rachel.

Rylan snapped back from the image. Where the hell had that come from? She burst shakily to her feet. Memories of her afternoon with Birdie morphed into an instant image of her daughter. The guilt grew, pulling at her with sharp hands. Ashamed, and not entirely sure why, Rylan slapped her hand on the night table, looking for her iPad. Moments like this called for a little therapist-friend e-mail connection.

Was it possible her subconscious was afraid Rachel's memory would be pushed out? Replaced? Rylan froze. She could never replace her daughter's memory. Yet if she continued to allow herself to get close to Birdie, maybe the moments she had with Birdie in the present would override the memory of those she'd had in the past with Rachel.

She would be replaced… Was that even possible? And if it was…

The bedside table where she kept the tablet was empty. With a groan, Rylan remembered she'd left it on the dining room table earlier. Human company was the last thing she wanted right now, but considering how quiet the house was, Rylan figured everyone had likely retired for the night. She padded down the hall barefoot, stopping dead when the living room came into view.

Cole was on the leather couch, Birdie tucked into his arm while he read to her. Rylan's chest swelled when she saw them there. Tucker lounged sideways in a chair in the corner, hat pulled low over his face, soft snores rumbling off him. The Haywoods were rarely in the house together, and when they were, it was never this quiet. The simplicity of the moment was warmth and disconcertment rolled into one prickly ball. She preferred the chaos of daytime. It helped her remember that family was just what she was trying to forget.

Discomfort made her tiptoe as stealthily as possible to the table to grab her iPad. As much as she craved Cole's touch, she didn't want his attention right now. Not when her mind was racing and her heart was being pulled in different directions. Relieved no one seemed to notice, Rylan turned covertly on one socked foot, ready to slink back down the hall, when the leather couch squeaked and Birdie's blond head appeared over the back.

"Ry, will you read?" Birdie climbed on her knees to stare. Cole sat up straighter. An appreciative smile crossed his lips, making her tingle everywhere but doing nothing to stop her fear.

Rylan shook her head and started to scoot back to the hall. "No, no. You read with your daddy."

"Read about the puppies!" Birdie patted the back of the couch, her braid flopping over one shoulder.

The tablet felt heavy in Rylan's hands, her socks itchy and tight. It was just one story. Mouth dry, she tried to smile, but her lips went hard and thin. She'd rather scrub the toilets with her own toothbrush than read to the round-faced, blond imp sucking on the back of the couch with pleading turquoise eyes. She'd had Birdie time today, and it was threatening to undo her.

Cole gently tugged Birdie's braid. "Come on, squirt. Let's finish this book."

"Ry, do it." The sharp protest stabbed Rylan in the throat. "Ry" didn't want to do it. Cole groaned and rubbed his eyes with a thumb and forefinger.

"Birdie, baby, it's late. Daddy's tired. Can we—"

Birdie swiveled on the couch, slapping the cushion. "C'mon, Ry."

A nugget of longing poked through the hesitation and made her take a step to the couch. Chest tight, hands tingly, Rylan found herself next to Birdie. She set the tablet down and took a seat a good foot away. Birdie bounced on her butt twice, her gauzy pink nightdress fluttering around her legs. A thumb in her mouth, Birdie edged a little closer.

Rylan's back was painfully straight. She cleared her throat, hoping Birdie wouldn't decide to flop into her lap. Cole tossed the book with a wink, and it landed on her tightly knit hands. Rylan jumped.

"Daddy, you lost the page!"

"Sorry, baby."

Birdie wiggled on the couch again, the ruffle of her nightgown touching Rylan's thigh. Rylan held her breath, watching from the corner of her eye as Birdie leaned over to look at the book. When Rylan still didn't read, Birdie leaned closer, her hair brushing Rylan's forearms. Her skin prickled from the contact. Freshly washed little-girl scent paralyzed her. Lavender soap, baby lotion—all that was missing was the sweet dust of baby powder.

"There!" Birdie punched the page with one finger before folding her hands patiently in her lap. Rylan looked at the page. Shallow breathing made it hard to get the words out. She tried. Her voice cracked. She tried again but no sound would come.

Rylan glanced at Birdie. Blond hair, big blue eyes. Not blond hair and big brown eyes. Long, almost-a-preschooler legs, not pudgy baby legs. Cole's scent reached her, sun-warmed skin, sweat, and crisp, sporty deodorant. No day-old-alcohol or fresh-scotch smell anywhere. The room squeezed around her, and suddenly she was on another couch with another man, another child. In another lifetime.

"Read," Birdie encouraged, kicking the couch with her legs.

"Okay, Rachel." Pressure pounded her head as the name slipped out. Maybe it was quiet enough that no one noticed. Tears bit Rylan's eyes and filled her voice as she began to read about a puppy with a lost collar. The room was still, save the sound of her shaking voice.

Once she started reading, she couldn't stop. The words absorbed in her brain, came out her mouth in robotic, choppy tones. Birdie was staring at her.

"Jesus," Cole whispered. He leaned over and touched Rylan's hand. "I've got this." He plucked the book from her grip.

Rylan looked at him in question, realizing the pages were puckered from her tears. Horrified, Rylan wiped her wet cheeks. Spine burning, she grabbed the tablet and hurried from the room. The mattress came up to her face as she plowed onto the bed, chest heaving, pulling her into memories she'd never fully live again.

Chapter Thirteen

Rylan looked up from decorating cupcakes for Birdie's birthday party the next day to find a white envelope sliding across the counter in her direction. She flinched in surprise, thinking she was alone in the house. Tucker stood on the other side, a teasing grin on his face.

"I'll trade you this letter for that cupcake." He pointed to a miniature vanilla cake topped with buttercream frosting and colorful sugar butterflies. Rylan couldn't help but smile. Tucker and Cole looked alike, but Tucker was easygoing to Cole's tense and always had a ready smile to Cole's more serious nature.

"Depends on if you're trying to pawn junk mail off on me or not." She wiped her hands on a dish towel and reached for the letter. He tapped it on the counter, withdrawing it when her hand snaked over the counter. Rylan raised her brows in challenge and slowly slid the cupcake at him, blocking it by covering it loosely with her palm when he tried to grab it.

"Ah, well played." He tossed the letter down, grabbed the treat with an *mmm* sound that made her snort. There had to be a thirteen-year-old trapped in that big, muscular body. Observant of the way he continued to eyeball the remaining cupcakes, Rylan moved them out of his reach as she flipped the envelope over. The law office's logo caught her eye immediately, and by the thickness of what was folded inside, she wasn't sure she was going to like what it contained. The ruling on the case against her could come at any time.

She looked at it, sweat breaking out along her hairline. If it was bad, wouldn't her lawyer have called? He was letter-happy and usually corresponded with her that way, and until right now, she'd been fine with that. No news was good news, and she hadn't had any news since the last correspondence, which had been a bill and not actually information.

"Everything okay?" Tucker licked frosting from his fingers.

"Mmm-hmm," she replied, taking off her apron. "Ah, Birdie is napping and Maeve is in the office. Mind if I take a minute?"

"I'll hang around for another cupcake." Apparently, she should have made Tucker his own batch. She handed over a chocolate cake this time, wagged a warning finger at him not to take any more, and slipped out the back door. The letter stared at her from the passenger seat of the truck as she went down the driveway, found a path that veered to the right and took it, wanting space between herself and civilization. If the news was bad, she was going to need a minute — or one hundred of them — alone.

She parked in the middle of the field. She took a few deep breaths as she flipped the radio until a rock station came in clear. She cranked the volume, the truck vibrating with the boom of bass and screaming vocals. The music quelled her anxiety just enough that she could breathe and rip open the letter.

Rylan,

I'm glad to tell you that the Martin family has dropped the civil suit against you. After taking time to grieve and process what happened, the family felt you were in no way responsible for your husband's actions and have been through enough trauma with the deaths of your husband and child. They asked me to pass along their condolences and best wishes.

This means that no further legal action can be taken against you, and your financial assets are your own. I hope this helps bring peace and healing to you, as well, Rylan. Please call me if you feel the need.

All the best,
Harry Latimer

Relief came with a hefty dose of nausea. The letter crumpled in her hand while she cried. No more lawsuits. No more threatening legal letters. It was settled. She hadn't done anything to the victim, but her husband's actions had given Rylan some measure of guilt by proxy. Harry hadn't thought the case would be ruled in the Martins' favor, but they had to take it seriously, go through the motions. And she'd had to live with the constant reminder, the constant threat, that her past would strip her of her future.

Her savings would have been gone, her credibility as a police officer further soiled. She'd already been snubbed in Madison as the wife of the judge who'd committed vehicular homicide. Then when a prostitute had come forward and exposed his taboo extracurricular activities, Rylan's chances of ever working in law enforcement in the district had disappeared completely.

The music cycled through three songs while she slumped in the seat, hand to her forehead, crying. It felt good to cry, to get it out. Rylan let the next song play to the end before clicking off the radio. The absence of music made her ears ring with silence.

"Not the type of music we usually listen to around here." The deep voice made her jump and hit her head against the window frame. Cole leaned over the saddle, looking in the truck window. The music had been so loud she hadn't heard him ride up. He was shirtless, chaps and dark jeans hugging his legs, the damn hat tipped over his forehead.

"Jesus, Cole, you fucking scared me." Rylan wiped at her wet cheeks, but hot tears were still spilling over. She turned away, though there was no doubt Cole had seen them.

"Hmmm, listen to that language from our favorite housekeeper." His playful smirk didn't help the struggle inside her. "Want to tell me about it?" Cole backed the horse up a little.

"How'd you know I was here?" Rylan crossed her arms and sniffed. Cole's face bunched in what might have been sympathy. His bare arms crossed over the pommel, his chest muscles bulging.

"I didn't. Was riding the fence and saw the truck." Cole dismounted and leaned an elbow on the open window, surrounding her with the scent of masculine sweat, horse, and dust. She closed her eyes with a shake of her head. Fresh tears overwhelmed her, and she buried her face in her arms.

This was when most men ran away, and Rylan fully expected him to leave her—wanted him to—so she could let it all out on her own.

Instead he flung the truck door open and pulled her out, straight up against his chest and into his arms where her face found the comfort of his sun-kissed and work-slick skin. And there was no place she'd rather be. All the struggles over internalizing everything faded as Rylan sank into the sheer power of his body and his willingness to support her. Cole stood steady, breathing with her until the panic passed, even his heartbeat encouraging hers to slow, to just trust him. And she did. He made it impossible to do otherwise.

And then he was kissing her hair and smoothing tears from her cheeks with his thumbs. "Ah, sweetheart," he whispered. "What's wrong?" That he even cared, when they'd sworn to be nothing more than willing bed partners, made her cry harder.

"I'm just so relieved," she finally managed. He was quiet while she struggled to regain control. It didn't matter if she shared this with him anymore, she supposed. Where she'd wondered before what he'd think about her if he knew, it didn't matter now. She was cleared.

"Why?" He took her hand. The cleft in his chin was hidden by dark, day-old stubble, but she knew it was there and wanted to touch her finger to it. His eyes blazed ocean green, brilliant against his tan skin and the dark wash of ebony hair that whisked from beneath his hat and fell over his brow.

She took a deep breath and wiped her cheeks. "I was being sued for half a million dollars." The golden tan of Cole's face blanched. Rylan sniffed and hurried on. "My husband got drunk and killed himself and an eighty-year-old grandmother when he crashed head-on into her Saturn. Her family had a civil suit against me but decided to drop it." She took a step back, her fingers curling around his hand.

"Holy shit, Rylan—"

"There's more." She swallowed the bile that rose in her throat. His fingers squeezed hers. No sense in only telling him half of it.

"Okay…"

"Our eighteen-month-old daughter, Rachel, was in the car with him."

Cole's hand fell away. Rylan cupped her mouth and turned to the truck, barely believing she was telling him. She'd wished before that she'd been strong enough to tell him—it seemed important somehow—but the time had never felt right.

"Rachel had gone to day care two half-days a week. I'd usually picked her up, but the car wouldn't start that afternoon, so Peter picked her up after a case at the courthouse. He'd said they were going to go shopping, but he ended up drinking a bottle of vodka while he drove around in the car…with Rachel inside." She shook her head, pinching her lower lip between her thumb and forefinger as the memories came on instant replay in her brain.

"After I found out about his hooker obsession, I asked for a divorce. But he… He threatened to have me blackballed from law enforcement, would use his money and his power to ruin me and take Rachel away. He was going to take my daughter away from me. Despite everything he'd put us through, I wasn't strong enough to stand up to him."

She turned to Cole. He was rigid, his hands hanging at his sides, motionless. Expressionless.

"I should have just left him. I should have been brave enough to walk out the door with Rachel and not care what he might do later. But I didn't… She died that night, and he did exactly what he promised. He left me with nothing."

Before she could inhale, Cole pulled her hard against his body and crushed her with his arms crossed over her back. His chest and abdomen clenched in a long, hard exhale.

"Jesus Christ, Rylan. I don't… I can't even…" His cheek pressed against the top of her head, his arms tightening until her ribs started to ache. She clung to him, and they were silent for a long time. When his arms finally loosened, she glanced up to see heavy sadness in his eyes.

"I can put the lawsuit behind me, but a big part of me feels like I deserved to lose. Like it was a punishment for not being strong enough. I took a bullet to bring justice to four women I had never met the night I brought the rapist down. But…I wasn't strong enough to stand up to him for my own daughter's sake."

"Stop. Rylan. Stop." Cole's fingers threaded through her hair as he placed a warm kiss on her brow.

Her insides melted at his gentleness, her heart aching for him. God, she could love him so easily—just fall right into him and hang on tight. If only she could… Emotions were turning her thoughts into uninhibited and uncontrollable word salad. Even if she'd tried to hold back her inner feelings, it wouldn't have worked.

"It would be so easy to fall in love with you, Cole. I thought that maybe once I put this lawsuit behind me…that if we ever decided to take it further, I *could*." He turned to stone, even his chest hitching and holding. "I would let myself, but I can't." She touched his jaw, the contact seeming to jerk him from his stupor. He grabbed her wrist lightly.

"Why?" The simple question told her that he'd thought about taking it further, too.

Rylan clenched her eyes as tears fell. "Because I can't ever be a mother again."

Pins and needles assaulted Cole's scalp and raced down his spine. He stared at her, knowing he should say something. Why wouldn't words come? His mind was reeling from everything she'd confessed. The empty feeling he'd gotten from the heavy anguish in her voice when she relayed how Peter threatened to take Rachel away was getting worse.

He was going to use his money and his power to take her away.

A tight clench made it hard for Cole to breathe as a wall of resistance built up inside. He wasn't going to think about the pang of familiarity—and surprisingly, the guilt—her words brought him. He thought of Livy and how easily she'd taken what he offered in exchange for Birdie. He wouldn't feel guilty about that.

He met Rylan's gaze, knowing she was expecting some kind of reaction from him. The truth was he didn't know exactly how he felt just then. There were so many things— relief that her legal troubles had nothing to do with deviance on her part, joy that she'd trusted him enough to share her secrets with him, a sudden hope over the idea of having her love, fear that his past would turn her away. And then, the realization that it didn't matter because she'd just said she couldn't be a mother again.

If there wasn't a place for Birdie in her heart, there wasn't a place for him either.

Rylan's throat moved as she swallowed hard. She lowered her eyes, and he knew she realized he was at a loss for words.

"Do you mean that you physically can't have any more children? Because, that's—" Rylan shook her head to interrupt him.

"I mean, I can't...in here." She put a hand over her heart, fresh tears glistening in her eyes. The empty cavity in him filled up with weights, dragging him down. He wanted to understand, but the baser side of his brain, the one that needed to protect Birdie, wouldn't allow it.

"I'm scared, Cole," she whispered. "I'm scared that if I let Birdie in, I'm going to forget Rachel."

"Oh, hell." Her words were raw and they killed him. No wonder she'd melted down while reading to Birdie last night. He should say something to comfort her, reassure her, but he couldn't. On numb legs, Cole turned his back. He took a deep breath, confused and dumbstruck at the same time. Birdie was already attached to Rylan. All he could envision was Birdie falling completely in love with Rylan, and Rylan walking away.

Fuck. She'd walk away from them both because he was one little jump away from being in love with her himself. Her breath shuddered behind him, and a heavy sting pushed behind his eyes. He couldn't let Birdie's little heart be ripped out. He just couldn't.

"Please, Cole. Say something."

He reached for the horse's reins, gathered them in his left hand. Rylan gave a desperate gasp.

"Cole, please."

He refused to turn and look at her, just swung himself up into the saddle. "I can't, Rylan. I'm sorry."

He was the world's biggest asshole. He knew it as he rode off. But all he could think about was putting space between them before anyone got hurt.

Chapter Fourteen

"We've got to get up in the high pastures and bring the herd down." Tucker pulled his gloves off and threw them on the ground so he could untie a rope knot. The ranch's property ran far up into the mountain range, where scattered stretches of pastureland spread between the valleys and peaks. It was almost time to bring the herd down to closer pasture anyway, but the unusual storm system slated to hit their area in the next five days made it more urgent.

Cole braced a broken gate panel on a log so he could repair the bolts that held the brackets in place. Birdie's birthday was today, *now* to be exact, and Tuck wanted to talk about a two-day endeavor?

"If you want to round up a crew, go ahead. I'll have to sit this one out." Cole banged a wrench against the bolt, driving it into the bracket.

Tucker snorted while he looped rope. "Like hell you're sitting out."

Cole looked up, and they locked eyes. "Ma isn't doing well at all, if you haven't noticed. Who is going to watch Birdie while I'm up on the mountain?"

"Isn't that what we pay Rylan for?" Tucker coiled the rope and put it over his shoulder. Cole stood so fast, Tucker jumped back, Cole's head nearly knocking him in the nose.

"No, that's not what we pay her for!" Cole threw the wrench on the ground, a small tornado of dust welling up from the impact. "Don't mention it again."

Tucker leaned against the fence. "Can I ask why?"

"No!" Cole grabbed the wrench and resumed banging the bracket. The bracket that would have worked fine if he wasn't beating it to death now. He needed to hit something, and it was either Tucker or the gate. Metal bled and complained less.

"Dude…" Tucker laughed. "What the hell is going on with you two?"

"Nothing." Cole warned him with a look as Tucker opened his mouth. Cole pointed a finger. "Unless you want a split lip, I'd shut up right now." In true Tucker fashion, he stood to his full height, back straight and arms bulging. Tucker was built like some Neanderthal ancestor, and shit if he didn't like to use his size to impress and intimidate. Good thing Cole wasn't intimidated.

He stood and faced his brother, already sick of whatever this was. He just wanted the gate fixed and his personal life quiet, so he could get on with Birdie's party.

"Hell, Tucker, can we do this later? I've got things to do."

"Yeah, like getting those cattle down here pronto."

Cole shook his head in exasperation and gathered his

tools. Tucker was close behind as Cole dumped his gear in the barn and stomped off to the house. He was so worked up his neck muscles screamed with tension. Rylan and her confessions. Rylan and her tears. Rylan and her soft, supple, naked body. He hadn't stopped thinking of any of those things, stayed up most of the night aching to make it right somehow.

Cole slipped into the house as cars pulled into the yard. Knowing Maeve, she'd invited every cousin and friend of the family to come celebrate Birdie's fifth birthday. Before long, the place would be crawling with family and friends, and he'd be going nuts surrounded by all those people. But it would make Birdie happy, and for her, he'd endure it. Keeping his relationship with Rylan quiet in front of all those people would be harder when all he wanted to do was drag her off somewhere and find the right things to say.

He had no clue what to say. All he knew was that the thought of her hurting was tearing him up inside. He'd caused her hurt by walking away from her confessions, but he had to protect Birdie's interests. Knowing what exactly to apologize for and what not to had become a blurred mess.

Rylan came out of the kitchen with a huge tray of pink and yellow frosted cupcakes. He was standing right there— Cole knew she saw him—but Rylan didn't look up and she didn't acknowledge him. Her usually soft face was tight as she set the tray on the long dining room table and wiped her hands on her ripped blue jeans. Cole should have gone on to his room and his shower but he stayed where he was, watching Rylan sway back down the hall, returning a moment later with more cupcakes.

Streamers and bright-pink decorations hung all over the

dining and living room. The table was set in true little-girl party fashion. Seeing Rylan dusted with flour, remnants of frosting smeared on her old T-shirt, he had no doubt she'd taken care of most of the decorations and baking herself while Maeve rested. His brow fell as he looked around once more. He thought about the bear she'd helped Birdie make at the mall for Levi and the tender way she'd cared for Birdie when she'd been hurt. She'd done it all—for a child she claimed she couldn't let into her heart.

He moved so he blocked her way. She finally looked at him, frowned to see a puff of dust roll off his boots and onto the gleaming wood floor. She made a little half turn as if to avoid him but Cole reached for the tray.

"I'll take those." That got her attention.

"No!" Rylan swerved the tray out of his reach. "Your hands!" Cole wiped his grimy hands on his jeans and took the tray, despite her protest. He set the tray next to the other, turned to follow her as she walked into the hallway. His hand found her wrist.

"Look at me." His hand slid up her arm and over the tendon of her shoulder, relief flooding him at the warm feel of her body. Car doors slammed outside, the timbre of voices wafting in through the open windows. Rylan glanced around nervously at the sound. Her gaze flickered up at him for a moment, sadness heavy in her eyes.

He gave her a gentle but insistent squeeze. "You did all this for my daughter. Don't tell me that you don't care about her a little bit—"

Rylan glanced around, her voice rushed and low. "I didn't say that I don't care about her. I said that I'm—"

"How long did it take you to do all this? *Hours.* Hours

spent on making sure Birdie's party is beautiful."

He didn't know why desperation clamped so hard on his gut when Rylan shook her head. Confusion played across her face, her head tilting just a bit.

"Why does it even matter? It's not like we want a relationship, Cole." She blinked fast. "I mean, I thought we —"

Tucker came into the hall, a brown package in his hand. He stopped when he saw them, one foot in mid-step. Cole swore, let his hand drop from Rylan's shoulder.

"What?" he snapped.

Rylan spun and went down the hall to the back door. He tracked the sway of her hips until she was out of sight, held himself back from following her as the door opened and closed.

"Don't ask," he warned.

Tucker cleared his throat with an amused tone. "I won't, but I do ask that you don't swing at me when I give you this. It came in today's mail." Tucker thrust the package at Cole. "It's from Livy. For Birdie."

Cole grabbed the package as the outside deck filled with voices. Knowing he would be missed if he was late to the festivities, and not wanting to miss a moment of it, Cole stormed into the kitchen and tossed the package in the trash before he headed to the shower.

• • •

Birdie was still on a sugar high from the birthday cake, cupcakes, soda, and cookies at her party the day before. He looked at Birdie, his heart swelling at the sight of her little face. He sympathized with Rylan. How could he not? She'd lost her daughter, and that kind of pain was nothing he had experience with. He hadn't felt it when Livy left or when his father died. His grief had been more of a stabbing ache that pounded him in suffocating bursts and then went away, finally, fading altogether. But losing Birdie—that was agony he couldn't fathom. He had no doubt that it would kill him.

He tried to keep his mind off Rylan as they finished their errands, but every spare second, his thoughts strayed to the look in her eyes when she told him about Rachel, to the heartfelt ache in her voice when she confessed to being scared. He was scared, too.

Scared of how he hated every hour that passed that he didn't see her.

Scared of how hard his heart beat when someone said her name.

Scared she was going to walk away.

She was perfect for him and for Birdie. She was. He knew it in every quiet moment he'd had to reflect on the things he wanted—to build a home of his own, a family for Birdie. The thoughts included Rylan's hand in his until the day they put him in the ground. He'd been good at brushing it off, but he didn't want to ignore it anymore.

"Daddy?" Birdie tugged on his wrist. Cole glanced down—he'd stopped in the middle of the sidewalk of the strip mall. His pulse beat hard against his neck. When had this happened? His brain raced through an album of the moments he and Rylan had shared, flashes of the minutes and hours flickering like a faulty television. Even if he could have focused on one particular moment, it would have been the wrong one because there wasn't one *exact* moment. It was the accumulation of them all. They'd agreed to nothing more than what they shared in bed, but now feelings were creeping in. Big feelings.

The wonderful, warm, syrupy way he was slipping into love with her.

Oh, God.

"Daddy!" Birdie pulled harder this time. She jabbed her pointer finger to the window of the Western store. She loved fingering the fringed chaps and vests, and playing with tooled silver buckles and conchas. Cole rubbed his face and focused on his daughter. He grinned. She pulled him inside and made a beeline for the pair of red cowboy boots in the display window.

Her little hands snatched the tiny toddler pair and hugged them to her chest. "Look!"

He bent to her level, prying one boot from her death grip. He could never say no to her. If she wanted the boots, he'd get her the damn boots.

"These are some red boots, baby." Bright crimson with a light-red thread used for floral-pattern stitching all over the boot shaft. Birdie wiggled off a sandal and shoved her foot into the wrong side. Cole shook his head and found a pair to size, then helped her try them on. He had to admit, his little blond daughter rocked those red boots. Without missing a beat, Birdie ran down the aisle to the adult section and found the same boots on the shelf.

"Ry's boots?" She struggled to pull a box down, nearly toppling over. Cole caught her with one hand.

"Whoa, there. You think Rylan needs boots?" Still a little shell-shocked over his realization of how much he was falling for her, a little plan formed in his mind. Birdie opened the box, pulling out a red boot with triumph on her face.

"Ry's boots!" One foot popped out and she held the adult boot next to her own. "See? They match!"

"They sure do, honey." He could imagine Rylan in the boots...just the boots. They'd look great with her summery tan skin, dark hair falling down her back. As much as he loved that idea, he had one better—let Birdie give Rylan the boots as a gift and, maybe, help her see that letting Birdie into her heart wouldn't be a bad thing. If she opened up a little more, he'd know that he was taking steps in the right direction with his growing emotion for her. If she resisted, he'd know to rein it in. Tonight, the three of them could spend time together, maybe take a ride and see what happened.

Even as he tried to solidify a plan in his mind, the fear that Rylan wouldn't be able to love Birdie spoke the loudest.

He guessed at Rylan's size and paid for both pairs of boots with a lightness in his chest he hadn't felt in a long time. Birdie clomped on the concrete, hugging the too-big box for Rylan in her arms. He knew she'd spill the beans the minute they pulled up to the house. Cole smiled as he buckled her into her car seat and headed out, listened to Birdie sing a song to her boots. As they drove to the feed mill to place an order, Cole tried to imagine Rylan's reaction to the boots. It was time to just let things unfold. And he hoped the loud voice in his head—the one full of doubt—was wrong.

Chapter Fifteen

Rylan leaned closer to the bathroom mirror to check her makeup, wishing she felt more enthusiastic about going out. Maeve's new medication seemed to be working, and she was eager to flex her newfound strength by venturing out a little. When she'd asked Rylan to join her and Jim Gilfoyle for dinner in Greenbrook, Rylan had eagerly accepted. But as time ticked on, she felt less and less like going.

The twinkle in Maeve's eyes when she spoke about Jim made Rylan pretty sure Maeve had some serious underlying feelings for him. It was sweet and agonizing to see her so obviously smitten and trying to hide it so hard. Rylan fingered her hair while staring at herself in the mirror. Her eyes seemed a little blank… Broken? She looked at herself harder, focusing more intently on the shadows in her eyes.

She was smitten and hiding it too. Hiding it because she had to. Because he didn't know just how much she was falling for him. Because it was against the rules for her to be involved with him in the first place. Even as she thought it, the strength of that taboo wasn't as potent as it used to be.

Rylan's brow fell as realization slid home. If that was her soul looking back at her in the glass, it was telling her it was time to complete the change. She'd come here to get better, to heal. She'd come here to find peace—happiness, even— and she had. But she'd found so much more.

Cole.

The way he'd touched her, the way she'd allowed it and gloried in it, felt so naturally fulfilling and satisfying. She hadn't craved his touch as a fill-in for all the pieces missing inside her soul. No, she'd wanted his hands on her, his lips on her skin, his body molding against hers, all of it, all of him, the way a woman does when she wants a man.

Rylan pulled back from the mirror but didn't look away. Rachel's image came to her mind's eye so easily, in a flash and with mostly complete recall every time she drummed a memory up. Even after she'd helped Birdie with a bath or showed her how to fold towels. Birdie's existence hadn't done anything to steal Rachel's memory, but could she trust it not to happen eventually?

Rylan brushed the thought away and grabbed the keys from her purse. There was no sense in dwelling on it. Frustration seeped into her. Cole hadn't come out and said how he felt about her, or what he really wanted from her. True, he'd hinted at it, led her round and round, and she was damn dizzy from not knowing. But there was no sense in even attempting to let Birdie into her heart if she and Cole were just fuck-buddies. Her heart fell at the thought. As perfect as their intimacy was, she didn't know if it would be enough, and it skewered her. She'd told him she wouldn't press him for more, that she didn't need more. But the more time she spent with Cole, the more she realized she was wrong. She wanted all of him, body and heart.

"Ry!" The sound of footsteps racing toward her room pulled Rylan away from her thoughts. She stepped out into the hall to see Birdie, a huge smile on her face, and Cole with a box under one arm. "You have a present!" Birdie grabbed the hem of Rylan's navy linen shirt.

Cole stopped behind Birdie, and Rylan held her breath for a fraction. His dark hair shone in the sunlight, his eggplant button-down and dark blue jeans a perfect accompaniment to his long, muscular body. The battered brown hat dangled from one hand, the tips of his black boots peeking out from the hem of his jeans. She remembered how incredible that day-old stubble on his jaw felt against her bare skin—

Birdie grabbed the box from Cole, threw it on the floor, and sat with it between her knees. "Open it!"

Rylan looked from Birdie to Cole, an uncomfortable flutter spreading in her chest. She checked her watch, hesitating. Cole's warm smile faded a little and Rylan's discomfort spread even more.

"You look nice," Cole said lightly. "Going out?"

"Open it!" Birdie hollered again, lifting the top of the box.

Rylan nodded. "I'm having dinner with Mr. Gilfoyle…" Cole's look of disappointment and blasé response cut her off before she could add, "and your mother."

"I see."

"Is that a problem?" Her hands hovered over the lid of the box as Birdie pushed it closer to her. Cole shook his head, all relaxation gone from his stance and expression.

"Ry, open your boots!" Birdie demanded. Rylan looked down and gave Birdie what she hoped was a smile that said "just a minute."

"I never said that." His arms crossed. If she didn't know better, she'd think he was jealous. Frustration burst through the surface, bringing everything else from the past few days with it.

"That's just it! You never said *anything*!"

Birdie shoved the box against her ankles. Rylan put a finger up to the child as Cole took a step toward her. His expression told her he knew exactly what she was talking about.

"What the hel—heck did you want me to say?" he whisper-shouted. "You told me you couldn't be a mother again, and I took that to heart, Rylan. As I pointed out at the birthday party, I don't think you're being honest with yourself. It's not up to me to realize, though—it's up to you."

Rylan crossed her arms and straightened her spine. She pushed out any hint of truth in what he said. Forcing her voice low and even, not wanting to do this in front of Birdie, but feeling powerless to stop it, Rylan rubbed two fingers to her brow.

"I hoped—" She shook her head.

"You hoped what?" His eyes were pleading, and her heart flipped to see it. Her gaze fell to his lips while her own parted and tingled, wishing he'd both move closer and go away.

"I just hoped you'd understand why I feel the way I do," she said quietly, eyeballing Birdie.

Cole's face was solemn, as though he'd been on the verge of something remarkable and stepped in a steaming pile of shit instead. Birdie was flipping the top of the boot box like a snapping alligator. He leaned over Birdie, patting her head with a soft hand. "Just a minute, baby."

Cole's hot breath washed over Rylan's neck as he leaned into her ear. His voiced gentled. "I do understand, Rylan. I do. But she already loves you, do you know that?"

"Daddy, give Ry her boots now?" Birdie scrambled to her feet and grabbed Rylan's leg. Rylan swallowed hard and forced her eyes away. There was no way she'd ever knowingly hurt Birdie—either of them. Rylan leaned back, Cole's searing eyes on her like a physical caress. She held out her hands for the box, and Birdie struggled to lift it up. Instead, Rylan knelt and opened it. Birdie moved the tissue paper aside with great fanfare and pointed, jumping up and down.

"See? Our boots match!" Birdie stuck one little red boot under Rylan's nose and wiggled it. The red boots inside the box were, indeed, a perfect match. Rylan took out one, her breath catching at the beauty of the craftsmanship and the cardinal color. Her lower lip trembled, despite her best attempt to hide it.

"Why…why did you get me these?" She gently grabbed Birdie's hand.

"Daddy said your flip-flops are—" Birdie glanced at Cole and bit her bottom lip before turning back to Rylan and whispering, "*crap*." Cole chuckled, the sound blowing away the ash in her heart.

Before a tear could let loose, Rylan gathered Birdie in her arms and hugged her. She tensed, expecting to feel anxiety at this closeness with Birdie, but there was none. It was just a sweet, simple hug.

"Try 'em on!" Birdie held out the other boot and wagged

it until Rylan slipped out of her ballet flats and into the boots. They were a perfect fit. Cole's thumbs were hooked in his pockets, the deep-purple shirt stretched nicely over his chest.

"Thank you," Rylan whispered.

Cole held his hand out to Birdie and gave Rylan a nod and a soft, lingering look. "Come on, Birdie. We don't want to make Rylan late for her date." Birdie bounced and grabbed her father's hand, clicking her heels on the floor.

"Ry looks pretty in her boots, Daddy."

"She sure does, baby."

And Rylan's heart cracked in two.

• • •

Rylan plopped the clothes basket on the love seat and then sat down next to it. The laundry room was too confining, and she hoped folding clothes in the bigger space would help her restlessness some. The open floor plan between the dining and living room gave Rylan a perfect early-morning view of the mountains from the French doors.

Since her run-in with Cole the night before, her nerves had been in a shambles. She smoothed and folded shirts, wishing she could go for a run, a long walk, anything to give her a break from the conflicting emotions warring inside her. She liked this family, all of them. A lot. When she lay in bed at night, surrounded by quiet, she could picture herself here, at Cole's side, a part of them. More, she could remove every-one and everything—the ranch, the cattle, the horses—and just have Cole and Birdie remain, and it was enough. In her heart, it was enough.

They were the family she wanted so badly.

The French doors in the dining room opened, letting the sun stream in. Rylan tossed a pair of folded socks into the basket and looked up. Straight into Cole's eyes. His stare was hard for a beat before he looked away. Birdie led Cole to the little white wicker table she'd dragged into the dining room last night. He sat dutifully. Within seconds, he had a tiny pink teacup in one grubby hand. Birdie gave him a white paper napkin and sat a teddy bear on his lap.

"Cross your legs, Daddy," Birdie chided.

Cole grunted. "I'm not a girl, Birdie. Only girls cross their legs."

"But you have to have manners."

Cole crossed his legs and pretended to drink from the cup.

"Not yet!" Birdie snaked a hand to his arm with a frown. Cole put the cup down. His long body stuffed into the little chair made Rylan wonder how he was going to get out without breaking it to bits. Cole gave his daughter all the attention she craved and then some. He glanced up at Rylan once more before turning back to Birdie, who was oblivious to Rylan's presence across the room. She watched them eat pretend cookies and drink water from little cups. Then came a plate of sloppy peanut butter and jelly sandwiches, and Rylan knew where the mess in the kitchen had come from.

"Grape?" Cole said with a faux frown. "You know I only eat strawberry jam." He winked.

"Ry likes strawberry." Birdie giggled. Cole grunted. Rylan smiled to hear herself woven into the conversation. When Birdie dabbed Cole's mouth with a napkin, her heart melted a little more.

The only thing that would make Cole sexier at this moment was a wedding ring.

Rylan stopped folding laundry as that little gem burst into her mind. It was a symbol of commitment and love, all the things women craved. She'd just never expected to see Cole in that light. Her brow crinkled. He'd already been down that road. So had she, and it hadn't worked out for either of them. As blurred as the lines were between her and Cole, thinking about more than the sparks-flying sex between them was a setup for pure disaster. She grabbed a handful of socks from the basket. Wasn't it?

Cole set his plastic cup down with a *clunk*. "Birdie, Daddy and Uncle Tuck have to ride out for a couple of days. Auntie Penny can't come get you because she got sick. You need to stay here with Grandma and Rylan." Cole struggled to sit straighter in the tiny chair. He patted his knee and Birdie flew onto it. Her little arms wrapped around his neck, and he kissed her hair.

"I come, too."

"No, baby. We're going to peak at the high pastures. It's not safe for you to ride that high up with us."

"But—"

Cole tapped Birdie's nose with a finger. "Promise me you won't do what you did last time." Rylan paired socks, wondering what had happened last time. Birdie squirmed on Cole's lap before burying her face in his neck. Rylan heard mumbling but couldn't make out the words. Then, Cole rubbed her back in little circles and said, "That's my good girl."

Cole stood and helped Birdie clean up the tea. "When I get back, I'll take you shopping. Grandma says you need a new quilt. You can pick something out, all right?" The deep timbre in Cole's voice made Rylan's skin tingle. He could lead a drove of angels straight into hell with that smooth, reassuring voice.

Birdie jumped up and down, shouting about princesses and horses and getting new curtains, too. Rylan resumed folding, disappointed when the duo left the room.

She snapped a towel and did it again just to hear the sound. Cole was the perfect father. Doting, attentive, protective. No matter how busy Paint River was on any given day, he'd come in to have breakfast with Birdie, even if it was just a cup of coffee. He'd read to her most nights, tucking her into his armpit and cuddling her close. More than once, Rylan had found them both asleep on the couch, Cole's head lolled off the edge, Birdie curled in a tiny ball at his side. It was painfully beautiful.

Envy and jealousy raged bright and hot, and Rylan struggled to stomp them down. She had no right to feel that way about what Cole and Birdie had, but she did. Peter had been attentive to Rachel only when it fit into his schedule or proved convenient. He'd never gone out of his way to hold her when she cried or soothe her or take her comforter shopping. All the emotional work had been left to Rylan, and when Rachel died, the spine of Rylan's emotional skeleton was ripped from her soul.

The moment Rachel's little body slipped out of her own in a tangle of blood and pain, Rylan knew she'd have the love she'd always craved. It was wrapped up in a squealing pink bundle, and the intensity of being a mother sustained her. It fed her soul and showed her what unconditional really meant. Cole understood that, too. She saw it on his face every time he looked at his daughter.

And Paint River was doing that for her now, wasn't it? She loved it here, loved the people. Though her time at the ranch had been short so far, it seeped into her in a way she'd hoped for but had not been expecting. Moving here to let life happen hadn't come with any guarantees, but it ended up being exactly what she'd been looking for. She felt grounded and needed, and had a purpose. Life here was simple but required hard work, and at the end of the day, her soul was full and satisfied.

That she'd found an incredible man was just an unexpected prize in the Cracker Jack box.

And she wanted to love Cole, to have him love her back. She wanted to let Birdie in. It might take a while, and she'd probably take a few missteps along the way, but she *wanted* it. Even if it meant quitting so Cole wouldn't be breaking any rules. Rylan's head snapped up at the thought. Quit? If it meant making things easier, she'd do it—move off the ranch, get a job in Greenbrook if it meant they could work on making their relationship into something more.

He was afraid that she was going to put Birdie through an emotional wringer, and Rylan didn't blame him. It might even stop him from wanting anything more. She sighed and paired two more socks. This was pointless. Until she knew what he wanted, there was no sense in trying to figure out how to make it work.

Rylan hurried through the rest of the laundry, glancing down at her new red boots. A lump welled up in her throat every time she looked at them. Finally done, she went upstairs to check on Birdie and found her reading with Maeve. A wave of tenderness went through her at the sight of the little girl tucked into her grandmother's arm.

"You okay if I go outside for a while?" Rylan asked. Maeve smiled, nodded, and waved her away. And then Rylan knew.

Chapter Sixteen

Cole reined his horse in behind the barn and pulled his gloves off finger by finger. Now that his tea party with Birdie was over, he was back to feeling ornery about going to the mountains tomorrow. And he couldn't get Rylan out of his head. Day or night, it didn't matter. His thoughts strayed to her with unwelcome frequency. He'd hoped to find someone again one day. *Just not someone with more emotional baggage than he had, that's for damn sure.* He'd ignored all his own rules and for what?

He wanted to believe he was inching toward another heartbreak, like what he'd had with Livy, but he refused. What he had with Rylan seemed more real, more solid, than what he'd ever had with Livy. Trepidation was still a strong contender in his heart, but what was stronger was the certainty, the odd way that he knew that Rylan was *the one.* If she didn't feel the same, there'd be no sense in worrying about it a minute longer.

The sky was cloudless and bright, but Cole knew that prettiness could turn deadly in the blink of an eye. They'd encounter snow when they made their climb up to the plateaus hiding in the mountain peaks tomorrow, and knowing Montana in August, she'd probably dump a few inches on them just because she could. If the weather turned shitty, there was no telling how long it might take to get back home. To Birdie.

To Rylan.

Cole's forehead bunched at the thought just as he looked up and saw Rylan walking toward him. His breath caught, and he knew no matter how much he'd been thinking about her, he wasn't ready for the rush of emotion making him tingle like a teenager.

She swayed a little as she sauntered over, the skirt of her blue chambray sundress swirling around the tops of her red boots. Her arms hugged a little white sweater close to her body, and her hair hung free around her shoulders like dark malt. Cole nudged his horse to meet her beside the barn. Her brilliant smile about unglued him right then and there.

"Hi." She walked up to the horse, grabbed the left stirrup and nudged Cole's foot out. He complied as curiosity burst through him.

"Hi," he replied cautiously.

"Mind if I come up?" Rylan put her right foot in the stirrup and reached for his right hand. Cole pulled her up as she launched herself into the saddle and sat facing him. His heart fluttered all over the place, nearly choking him with the force of it. He scooted back until his ass hit the back slope of the saddle. Rylan moved in easily, placing her thighs over the tops of his. Hands on his waist, she scooted forward until their pelvises wedged together, and she settled between his body and the pommel. Her sexy smile stole his breath as she hitched her thighs low around his hips.

Cole swallowed hard, his cock jumping to life at their fusion. "What are you doing?"

Rylan leaned in until her cheek brushed the side of his neck. Her arms slipped beneath his to embrace him, and Cole's blood roared. He glanced around, relieved to find they were alone. Trying to explain the "no fraternizing with employees rule" when Rylan was spread-eagled over his lap would be a little hard to do.

"Is there somewhere we can go?" she whispered, her lips brushing his earlobe once, twice before she took it between her teeth. "We have unfinished business." Rylan gripped his left hand and placed it on her thigh just beneath her skirt. She leaned back to look into his eyes, and Cole knew he was completely lost. He could barely breathe. She could do whatever the hell she wanted and he wouldn't say a word. She slid his hand up her silky leg, under the skirt and up, up until he cradled her round hip and followed the soft, panty-free curve of her ass. He searched her gaze as he felt her nakedness underneath. They did have unfinished business, but he'd imagined them talking about it, sorting it out. Rylan's plan was so much better.

"Rylan." Her name came out as a warning, an invitation, and a question all rolled into one. She touched his lips with one finger. A wild flame lit inside him with such intensity, he was tempted to throw her on the ground and fuck her right there. Cole paused for a breath, then another.

Rylan's fingers raked along his ribs. "Please?"

He couldn't deny her. Cole grabbed the back of her

head and ground their lips together. Rylan moaned beneath the fury of his kiss, her short nails digging into his back. She pulled away to smile at him, and the desperation he experienced at the loss of her lips really was ridiculous. Her hands cupped his face, and she kissed him softly, lightly at first. Then longer, with growing pressure and full-bodied heat that made Cole sink into himself. The sweet slide of her tongue against his was gut-wrenching, and he wanted more.

Cole's relaxed his grip, feeling anxiety morph into a delectable, deep ache. Her fingers flitted over his cheek, taking time to smooth over the planes of his face and curl under his jaw before branding fire down his neck. He pulled away from her lips, looped an arm firmly around her waist, and pulled her tight into him. One swift kick of his heels and the horse was off, taking him away from every reason he had to stop this now.

Rylan put her cheek on his shoulder and clung to him as they raced away. Time and miles passed with her soft breasts pressed against his chest, her strong arms curved around him in a warm embrace. The smell of her hair, the feel of her thighs on top of his—it was too much but not enough.

Cole slowed the horse as they came to the edge of a prairie lined with towering pines. Rylan reached for him as soon as the horse slowed to a walk, kissing him deeply, her lips seeking, tongue demanding. Her hips swayed in time with his to the gelding's gentle, lazy walk. Cole slid his hands under the dress, gripping her full hips with both hands and pulling her in tight, pelvis to pelvis. He was so hard and sensitive the contact of her body over his erection had him nearly careening off the horse. Her fast intake of breath when she settled over his cock didn't help. Cole threaded his fingers through her hair, made fistfuls. Her kisses turned softer, and he let her lead, wanted to follow so he knew just what she wanted. Just when he thought she was going to be gentle, Rylan crushed him in a bruising kiss—punishment of the most delicious sort.

Cole cupped her face and pulled back. Before this went any further, he wanted her to know that he understood her reservations, and how much he wanted to help her get past them.

"I'm humbled that you shared your past with me, Rylan."

Her hands came up to his wrists. "You are?" Cole cut her off with a kiss. Her hands slid to his chest, fingers tugging the buttons of his shirt, her movements desperate. As though she couldn't wait to get her hands all over him. Hell, he couldn't wait. Pulling back from her hips, he grabbed her wrists to stop her from tearing his shirt free. He was on the edge of so many things right now—falling deeper for her, falling into the dreams of family and peace he had at night. Not knowing if her heart would ever be big enough for his daughter, though, held Cole right there on the crumbly precipice.

He brought her right hand to his lips and kissed her knuckles, flipped her hand and trailed hot kisses over her palm. Her chest heaved with soft little pants, and when he loosened his grip on her, Rylan's arms went right back to his shirt, ripping it from his chest.

Cole groaned, pulling her sweater off and tucking it behind the saddle with his shirt. The straps of her sundress lowered easily. Rylan simply shrugged the straps off and the dress fell to her waist. He exhaled in a rush at the sight of her full breasts, dusky nipples hard and ready for his touch.

He palmed them both, squeezing and kneading the round flesh, awed by how incredible she felt in his hands. Rylan arched her back and leaned into him. Her fingers toyed with the back of his neck, running up into his hair and back down over his skin. Cole dipped his head to kiss her neck, her collarbone, and over her chest.

He pressed her back lightly, just enough that he could lift one breast in his hand. He took her nipple in his mouth, pulling it in deep. His brain rejoiced at the remembrance of her taste on his tongue. Rylan moaned, and his cock jumped in response. The taste of her skin made his tongue dance, the scent of vanilla perfume wrapping around him in sexy notes. He suckled the hard nub, pulling it gently with his teeth before swirling his tongue in slow circles. The steady motion of the horse rocked them both, Rylan's body swaying gently.

Cole shifted his attention to her other breast, lavishing it with kisses as her hands began a slow exploration of his body. A fluttery touch traced his pecs and over his abs, sliding around to the muscles of his back. Nails scraped over his spine and side, curving around his waist and back to his belly.

Cole's mind clouded with the density of complete and primal need. He grabbed Rylan's hips and tipped them up, encouraging her legs to relax so her thighs could fall farther apart. His lips found the soft curve where her neck sloped into her shoulder as he dipped one finger inside her. She was slick and hot and bucked so hard at his touch that Cole had to hold her tighter to keep her from falling. Intently, Cole ran his finger down her clit and back up, then again and again as Rylan melted in his arms. Her head rolled back, hands gripping his shoulders to keep steady.

"Cole!" Her eyes flew to his, and he grabbed her gaze as he pleasured her. He wanted to see every nuance cross her expression. A heavy veil of ecstasy clouded her eyes but she didn't look away. Rylan's eyelids twitched, her kiss-swollen lips parted in an expression of bewilderment that rocked him. He swore and stroked her faster so he could watch her come undone. He wanted to kiss her, hold her close, run his mouth down the length of her. But the craziness of doing *this* on the back of his horse left his brain cataloging all the things he'd do to her when they had more space, more time.

Rylan leaned back as far as she could, using his shoulders for support, her legs braced around him and her lower back pressed against the saddle horn. He felt a slight tremor in her thighs as her hips rose to meet his touch. Each movement of her pelvis rubbed against his cock, sending electric shocks through him. She was bared to him save for the bunched dress around her middle, the sight of her full breasts and open thighs the beauty of his dreams. But she was here, in his arms, coming under his hand, begging him with her body for more. Oh, and he'd give her more. Fuck, he'd give her anything right now just to see the passion cross her face over and over.

Her head flew up, and she crushed into him with a cry. Cole embraced her with his free arm, cradling her against his chest as her thighs clenched. Her body closed around his hand as deep, tangible tremors pulsed through her and quivered against his fingers.

"God, Cole!" Rylan's eyes closed, her head falling back just enough that he could see her expression as the orgasm rocked her. He'd never seen anything so sexy in his life. Before he could catch his breath, before he could think, her hands were unbuttoning his jeans and sliding the zipper down. His cock sprang free into her hand. Rylan rolled the tip between her fingers before stroking his length.

"Jesus," she said, palming him and wrapping her hand around him. "I want this now. Right now, Cole." He opened his jeans as far as they would go and hitched her up by her hips. With a frustrated growl, he stopped.

"No condom."

It took her a second to process why he'd stopped, her lips curved in protest. Then a flutter of her eyelashes. "I'm on the Pill." Their eyes caught and held. The reassuring nod she gave him was all he needed.

"Bend your knees over my thighs." Supporting her with his hands, Cole helped Rylan straddle him. She settled over him, meeting his eyes as he brought her down, his cock driving into her slowly, inch by inch. He bit his lower lip to keep from crying out. She was tight and slick, her sex stretching around him and cradling all of him until he was buried to the base. Rylan's arms encircled his neck, her cheek hot against his. Cold shocks scattered over his body like a spray of ice water that froze and burned on contact.

"Wait," he growled. God knew he needed a minute. "Feel the horse. Let it rock you." Cole held back the nearly uncontrollable urge to thrust. He took a deep breath, felt her relax. Goddamn, she felt so good. He sank into the rocking of the horse's gait, feeling Rylan's hips do the same. When he knew she had her balance, Cole gently lifted her hips, bracing himself as he brought her back down. Her hands gripped his shoulders for support as she settled into the sway of the horse. Her body found a rhythm, moving tortuously slowly up and down his shaft. Their motions were a little awkward in the cramped saddle with his jeans and her skirt in the way, but it was perfect. It was goddamn perfect.

He brought a hand to her hair. Rylan's head was tilted back, her lips parted and eyes closed with a flushed abandon that squeezed his heart. He wanted her to have every sweet sensation possible, didn't want that look to ever leave her face. He ran his fingers through her hair, left her just that amazing way.

Her body tightened around him, the cadence of her passion music to his ears. He must have made music of his own because she rode him faster, deeper, grinding down and encouraging him with perfect timing until his cock swelled so hard it rippled with pleasure-pain. Her face tipped down; she caught his eyes, her perfect pink lips quivering.

Rylan cried his name and he lost it. He gripped the back of her neck with one hand, the other digging into her hip, holding her steady as he thrust up hard and pulsed into her body. Cole's mind went black with the force of his body releasing in hard, rocking waves. Rylan's soft murmuring brought him back to the sweet reality that he was still buried inside her. She snuggled up against him, warm and soft. The horse stopped and they held each other, chest to chest, breath to breath.

Cole buried his face in her hair and swallowed down a flicker of fear. This wasn't just amazing sex. He was losing his heart. Fast.

The horse walked slowly beneath her, the sound of trickling water pulling Rylan from a satiating post-sex fog. She lifted up from Cole's shoulder to the glare of bright yellow sunlight bouncing off the rippling water beside them. His hand ran over her arms where she held him tight around the middle, the calluses on his fingers sending scratchy little shocks across her skin. She glanced down to see colored stones blinking up from beneath the rippling surface of the water.

The horse splashed through the shallow edge of the river and snorted in seeming enjoyment of the cool water. Cole glanced over at her once, then again, leaning back to encourage a kiss that she willing handed over. The light in Cole's eyes made her heart soar. He was so gorgeous it hurt, and his touch—knowing him this way—tipped the scales between wanting to love him and being able to.

Rylan pulled hair away from her eyes, her thighs gripping the horse tightly as he made a sudden sidestep to avoid a pile of large rocks.

"Cole…" She trailed a hand down his spine, smiling when he shivered. "I want Birdie." That wasn't exactly how she'd planned to bring it up, but it was close enough to the truth.

The horse stopped, and Cole threw his right leg over the front of the saddle, then jumped down. He turned to face her, one hand going to her thigh. "What?"

Insecurity started a rave in the middle of her self-confidence. What if he didn't want more and she ruined what they had? Rylan moved forward into the center of the saddle, her thighs aching in a sweet reminder of what they'd shared.

"I want to let Birdie in." She didn't know if that made sense, but the flicker of understanding on his face told her it was clear enough. Rylan leaned down a little, sliding her hand over his on her leg.

"What if you can't do it?" His fingers squeezed hers in

a bid for understanding. "What if I allow myself to fall completely head over heels in love with you, but in the end, you can't love Birdie?" Then he'd be broken, and she'd be responsible. No way did she want that for him, for Birdie or herself. "I know you're scared, Rylan, but so am I." Cole reached up and brushed hair away from her shoulder, the seriousness of his expression eating through the comfort of the intimacy they'd shared. The only response she could muster with all the arrows in her heart was a shake of her head.

"I don't blame you, Cole. I just wanted to know how you might feel about that."

His fingers gripped her knee, sending little shocks over her leg. "I want you." His thumb and forefinger pressed together against his lower lip. "If you feel—truly feel—that you're ready for us, then I am, too."

Rylan's body went weak as a sob built in her chest. She wanted to slip off the horse and throw herself in his arms, but she didn't. The look in his eyes was too beautiful to lose contact with, so she cupped his cheek with her hand and nodded, swallowing down the last of the insecurities she had over taking this leap.

"I can quit Paint River," she said. "If it'll make it easier, I'll do it."

Cole's brow furrowed, his fingers wrapping around the balls of her shoulders. "Hell, no. We need you. My mother needs you. *I* need you here." Cole scooted her forward in the saddle and swung up behind her, pulling her against him so tight she could barely breathe.

"You're staying put at the ranch. No way in hell am I losing you now, Rylan."

Chapter Seventeen

Rylan had to stretch high to reach the clothesline, pinning flat sheets and pillowcases in one long, fluttery row. The laundry made a nice barrier between her and the blazing sun, the wind teasing and tickling the fabric so it bobbed around her. Her time with Cole this morning might as well have been a lifetime ago. Only four hours had passed since they'd returned and managed to slip back into their workday quietly, but the ache in her chest told her it was four hours too long.

They'd certainly rounded a corner that changed everything, and the happiness that pumped through her was new and exciting and so very, very welcome. Maeve and Birdie had lain down for a nap a while ago, leaving Rylan to relish the quiet business of hanging laundry—the perfect task for replaying every word, every touch, every moment of the morning.

Rylan snapped a pillowcase before placing it up on the

line. She hummed as she worked, the random tune blending in perfectly with the stillness that filled her heart and mind. A figure casting a shadow behind the yellow sheet made her jump. She'd been so engrossed in the moment she hadn't heard anyone come over. Arms pushed through the sheet, wrapping around her, sheet and all.

"Get over here and kiss me," Cole said, his face pressing into the fabric and leaning in close. Rylan giggled, trying to shift away from his yellow-cotton-covered embrace. When that didn't work, she swatted his hands.

"No, I'm working!"

"I don't care. Kiss me anyway." He let go and swept the sheet aside, got stuck in the layers, and pulled the sheet down, clothespins flying, until it lay in a crumpled heap. Indignation at having to rewash the sheet burned away when he grabbed her good and proper.

"Kiss. Me." His hands pressed into her lower back, dipping her slightly as his fingers spread across her sensitive skin.

"Okay," she whispered, lips parting in anticipation. His breath bathed her lips, zings of electricity dancing on the tender flesh, calling out to her with the heat of his mouth. Rylan wrapped her arms around his neck, pillowcase dropping from her hand. His skin was warm and damp with sweat, the familiar feel of his flesh and muscle like coming home.

Cole pulled her up to her tiptoes, drawing a long kiss, his tongue gliding along hers and sweeping the corners of her mouth. When she groaned low, his teeth took her lower lip and pulled back gently so the tender flesh slipped through slowly. Her breasts ached in response, and she leaned closer.

"Miss me?" His lips left her mouth to tease her neck,

one hand sliding between them to find her breast. His thumb and forefinger pinched her nipple through her clothes. White light turned to shards behind her eyes.

"Hell, yes." Rylan leaned back, fingering the fringe of hair at the base of his neck. Goose bumps raced to life beneath her knuckles.

Cole palmed her breast harder this time, made little circles over her nipple with his palm. "I want your sexy legs wrapped around me." Both hands slid to her waist, his hands clamping her curves in with a possessive grip. "Tonight."

Rylan shivered at the word, so filled with promise. *Yes, tonight.* She pulled his head back down with a longing sigh.

Boot stomps racing across the ground accompanied a haughty female voice. "Cole Cooper Haywood, *really*?"

Cole jerked away so fast Rylan nearly fell to the ground. He spun, one hand still holding on to her waist. A tall blonde stood a few feet behind him, her crisp white capris and tangerine shirt, oversized black sunglasses, and dangling gold earrings making her worthy of a yacht luncheon. It only took a moment for Rylan to recall this woman as the same one Birdie had almost bumped into at the mall. The woman's eyes swept Rylan up and down with a smirk while she adjusted the big, square leather bag on her arm.

Tucker stood a few feet away from her, hands on his hips. He gave a sarcastic wave of his hand. "Oh, Cole, Livy is here."

Livy pursed her lips and bobbled one finger at Rylan. "Aren't you the woman I met in the mall?"

Cole released Rylan's shirt and took a step forward, shifting so he covered Rylan with his body. "What the hell are you doing here, Livy?" He righted his hat. His back went rigid, a muscle jumping low in his neck.

"Excuse her please, and I'll tell you."

Cole's head hitched a little to the side, his fingers bunching into fists. Rylan swallowed hard. He was almost crackling with rage. Rylan stepped to Cole's side and untied the half apron holding the clothespins from her waist. She wasn't one to back down from an insult. Rylan was about to move forward, but Cole pushed her back with a palm on her belly.

"You're pretty haughty for someone who used to scrub the cabin toilets." Cole's words pushed through gritted teeth. "Off the property. Now."

"Wait, I'm sorry." Livy held up a palm. "I'm just… frustrated, and I got worked up. You haven't called me back, and time is running out for me."

Livy removed her glasses and reached inside the glossy leather tote to produce a large manila envelope. She wagged it for Cole to take. He crossed his arms in blatant refusal. Rylan looked at Tucker. His face was stony, his arms also crossed over his chest like a sentinel. The imposing, hard stances of both men sent Rylan's shit-meet-fan-ometer on high alert.

"We're divorced. Everything is settled."

Rylan's stomach dropped. *This is Cole's ex-wife?*

Livy's shoulders softened just a touch, and Rylan was pretty sure her plump lower lip trembled just a bit.

"This doesn't have any legal involvement, Cole. It's… personal. Can we maybe go inside and talk?" She let her hand with the envelope drop to her side. Tucker eased up his stiff posture a little; Cole didn't.

"No."

Livy clenched her eyes and gave an irritated shake of her head before flipping a chunk of hair from her eyes with a pinky. "Stubborn as usual. Okay, look, even though I've been *calling* you and thinking about how to approach this, I'm still not sure how to really...spit it out."

A little pang hit Rylan at the hint of longing in Livy's eyes. "Two years after our divorce, I remarried. We've struggled with infertility, and just a few months ago, it was confirmed that I...can't have any more children."

Cole bristled harder. His neck veins popped, the tendons in his forearms straining against the skin. Rylan studied Livy's face, touched by the anguish she saw there.

"I'm not asking for Birdie back, so relax before that vein in your neck explodes," Livy said with a wave of her hand. Rylan let out a pent-up breath. Cole's eyes narrowed, but he didn't otherwise respond. The paper crinkled a little as Livy's well-manicured fingers dug into it.

"I made a mistake by walking out of her life." She daintily cleared her throat. "Given the circumstances—she's my only child, and I've never stopped thinking about her—I was hoping that, maybe, you'd consider letting her know me a little."

Livy's voice swelled with hope, pulling Rylan right along with it. She looked from Livy to Cole, searching him for some reaction, but the impassivity in his expression didn't crack. When he spoke, his tone was even, unemotional.

"You made your choice when she was born."

Livy's shoulders fell, a hand coming to her mouth. All the haughtiness seeped away, leaving behind a beautiful woman who looked utterly defeated. Rylan's heart tugged. Livy's expression called to her on some primal level, this longing and frustration in the woman's eyes. It was the look of a devastated, desperate mother.

Livy tipped her chin up, her nostrils flaring as she jabbed a finger in Cole's direction.

"That's right, Cole Haywood, I did. Your threat to use your money to drag me through the mud would have meant I lost her anyway, you son of a bitch."

Cole saw Rylan appear to sway out of the corner of his eye and turned just in time to support her by grabbing her elbow. Her face was blanched, lips pulled into a hard line. It only took one cursory glance at her expression to know what she was thinking. He tried to say her name, but nothing would come out as her small, firm hand pushed his away from her arm.

His throat was dry and tight, anger and concern over Rylan taking a toll on him. Until Rylan had told him about her husband's threats, he'd never thought twice about what he'd done to ensure he kept Birdie at his side. They'd gone to court and Livy had agreed to leave Birdie in Cole's care. In return for the flat settlement he'd quietly proposed, she had refused alimony and never made good on her court-appointed one-weekend-a-month visitation rights. Instead, Livy had taken the $350,000 in cash Cole had handed her and walked away.

In the years that followed, he'd worried that Livy would take advantage of the fact that she'd never signed off her parental rights, and as far as the law was concerned, she could ask the courts to revisit the custody agreement. As he lost himself in the total disbelief on Rylan's face, he'd never imagined that the under-the-table deal he'd made would come back to haunt him quite this way.

Livy had married him for money, had never had qualms about spending it and asking for more. He turned back to her, every part of him numb. "You were going to take Birdie to Texas. Hell, Livy, you had child support and alimony all planned out the day she was born. She was nothing more than a blank check to you."

Livy had recovered from her show of emotion and stood tall, though her face was softer, her eyes less venomous. She grimaced and looked at her feet. "I won't lie. Did I marry you for money, Cole? Partly. But it didn't take long to realize ranch life wasn't for me, and yeah, I wanted out and she was my ticket to keeping the lifestyle you'd given me. But when you offered the payout for Birdie, I figured it would be easier than trying to fight you in court for more. I just never realized how big of a hole would be left without her in my life."

Livy held the envelope out again with a shaking hand. "I'm not that person anymore, Cole. All I'm asking is to send her a letter now and then, and maybe have her send me a picture or two. Then, when she's older, if she wants to know me, I won't be a complete stranger. And if she doesn't, then that's okay, but at least I left the door open."

The grass rustled next to him as Rylan stepped away. Cole turned to her, wanting to grab her, but his legs still refused to cooperate. He was caught in an estrogen-fueled blender and had no clue how to get out. Rylan's eyes were cold.

His hand slid over his chest, palm flat against his heart. He blinked, Rylan's image blurring. "When Birdie was born, I knew what it *really meant* to love someone. She's all I ever

wanted… She's…she's mine. I couldn't let her go to Texas."
He managed to take one step toward Rylan, his hands spread
and pleading. "I know what you're thinking, Rylan, but goddammit, I'm not…I'm not Peter." His voice lost its velocity,
falling flat. He wasn't Peter, true. But he'd threatened Livy
the same way Peter had threatened Rylan, and right now,
he wasn't any better than Rylan's piece-of-shit husband had
been.

Rylan stepped backward, arms crossed, farther away
from him. "I just need…I'm—"

Cole's chest was on fire from the pleading bound of his
heart. *Please stay. Please, please stay.*

Rylan turned and hurried across the lawn, disappearing
around the side of the house. Cole whipped off his hat and
ran a hand over his forehead. Tucker caught his eye, gave a
little nod of reassurance, and followed Rylan's path.

Steeling himself against any new onslaught of feelings
that might want to further fuck with him, Cole reached for the
envelope in Livy's hand. She looked a little uncomfortable,
sympathetic even.

"I'm leaving for Germany in the morning. Carl's firm is
relocating him there indefinitely. My new address is inside,
in case you decide that my proposition is agreeable. I'd love
for her to send me something. Did she…did she get the gift
I sent?"

Cole rimmed the long edge of the envelope with his
thumb and forefinger. The gift he'd thrown in the trash that
Tucker had dug back out and put in Cole's room. Livy's sin-
cerity was hard for him to digest after so many years of re-
garding her as the woman who'd only wanted him for his
money. He'd been her ticket out of the trailer park—he'd

known before he'd even proposed. But he'd been so desperate for a family of his own that he'd been willing to take the risk. His marriage and his bank account suffered, but Birdie was more than worth it.

"I didn't give it to her yet." He was deflating by the second.

"Please, Cole. Think about what I've said." Livy hitched her bag higher on her shoulder and put her sunglasses back on. He'd been angry at Livy so long, it was hard to process that she sincerely wanted Birdie in her life, for more than just money. He'd think about it later. Right now, he had to fix things with the woman who'd walked away. Rylan had been willing to risk her still-healing heart on him. Now he needed to prove that he was worth it.

Chapter Eighteen

Driving through tears wasn't something Rylan had any experience with. It was harder than she'd thought, like driving through rain but without windshield wipers to take the blurriness away. No matter how many times she swiped at the burning little rivulets, new ones came. All this crying was turning her into a girl. Where was Rylan the cop when she needed her?

A parking lot came into view on her right, along with a broken neon sign flashing TAP. Whatever the word was in front of it, she couldn't tell. Making one last desperate slap at her eyes, Rylan parked next to the bar and killed the engine. When Tucker had raced after her back at the ranch house, Rylan thought he would try to stop her from leaving. Instead, he'd slipped twenty bucks in her hand and told her to get out of there for a while—to go to Greenbrook and have a drink. She had better things in mind, like coming up with all the ways she wanted to kill Cole Haywood for turning out to be a bastard.

A bastard she was in love with. A bastard who'd done to his wife exactly what Peter had threatened to do to her.

I'm not Peter, he'd said. *Right.*

The strains of country music rolled out of the small bar onto the street when she finally drummed up the nerve to open the bright-red door. What the hell, she'd gotten accustomed to having feelings since coming to Montana; she might as well make peace with bars, too, right? People milled in and out, a mixed crowd from what she could see, from college-age kids to men with graying temples.

She got carded at the door and felt good about it for a minute, then slipped into a chair at a small round table in the corner. The patrons around her laughed, talking and sloshing drinks. It was a rowdy crowd that hooted and complained when the DJ took a break and roared when he started playing again. Noise from the pool tables in the back mingled with the music, soft green light washing over her table from the overhead lights. The only thing missing were a handful of huge television screens playing Wisconsin Badgers football, as they had in every bar back home.

A waitress came by in a tiny black T-shirt. Hitching an eyebrow, Rylan had to squint to make out the silver lettering across the girl's boobs. TIT FOR TAP.

"Get you something?"

"A big stick and some duct tape?" Rylan had no idea where that came from. She must be finally ready to have that nervous breakdown. The quip did nothing to stop the pounding ache in her heart. The waitress just smiled and set a napkin down.

"Ah, boyfriend trouble, huh?" Trouble? That was one

way to put finding out the man you were sleeping with was a douche-canoe. Rylan nodded and said she didn't want anything at the moment—but that was mostly a lie. She wanted to know why life was doing this to her. Just when she'd started to let go and enjoy life—to let life fucking happen—Cole had to be...no different from her.

Rylan tapped her forehead with a finger as that little nugget took hold. How many times had she wished she'd had Peter's connections so she could turn the tables on him? She'd daydreamed many times about making his hooker fetish public, and she would have if she'd had hard evidence like pictures or something. She'd been too scared of what he'd do if he caught her digging deeper for proof.

The only difference between her and Cole was that he actually had the resources to do what she'd only fantasized about. Damn, that was bitter crow.

"Get you a drink?" A shadowy body slipped into the chair across from her. Rylan almost laughed at how young he was. His dark hair was parted on the side, and Rylan was pretty sure he'd ironed his T-shirt smooth. A frat boy through and through. She crinkled her nose to hold back a snarky reply.

"No, thanks." She hoped her curt response would discourage him but wasn't surprised when it didn't. His lower lip protruded with an easy smile while his hands cupped his beer bottle. Rylan noticed how smooth his hands looked in the soft bar light, how neatly trimmed and filed the nails were. So opposite from Cole's rough working hands...and so unappealing to her.

"You from around here?" He scooted the chair a bit closer.

"Maybe." She was just plain irritated now. Whatever rationalizations she'd been making with herself were slipping away. Frat Boy didn't catch on to the disinterest she put on her face. Beer-soaked bucks like him usually didn't. She'd had to intervene at more than her share of fights between stupid young college boys back in Madison.

"Thanks for the drink offer, but I need to get going." Rylan urged him to get out of her way with a nod of her head.

He laughed. "What's your hurry?" One manicured hand snaked over and gripped her knuckles. Big brown eyes looked hard into hers. Steely cold crackled in Rylan's veins. She was tired of being toyed with and done with holding back when she should be standing up for herself. The light of inebriation glowed bright, mixed with a fierceness that surprised her. A round of snickering came from her right. She didn't have to look to know his boy groupies were standing at the bar watching. The skin tingled at the base of her neck. The bar was getting more crowded by the minute, her path to the door blocked by a fresh string of bodies. For a moment, she had a flash of running through a crowded bar, her service weapon ready as she'd chased the rapist through the mass of bodies. He'd stopped against a wall, turned, and aimed...

Rylan tried to pull her hand back, but Frat Boy held tight. She cleared her throat calmly. "Let go." Where the hell was the bouncer who'd carded her at the door? It didn't matter, really. The hard-edge that had kept her sane through the shit of her career and personal life was still there, just waiting to be let out.

"Ah, come on, babe. Just one drink with me, huh?" He

leaned in. The stench of old beer washed over Rylan's nose and mouth. The tiny flame of anger inside her flickered brighter. She had no doubt she could handle this ass-wipe. It had been a while, but the I-am-woman-feel-my-fist part of her psyche that had kept her alive as a cop brewed to the surface.

"Nope," she replied. Rylan stood, her hand still captured in his. She'd never stopped being scared after one gunshot changed her life. She'd quit law enforcement after taking that bullet, had let it take her ability to be strong with it. Peter had capitalized on that, but no one ever would again. Moving carefully, Rylan slid the chair back with her foot. She tugged her hand again, still trapped.

"Here's what happens next," Rylan said evenly. "You're going to let go of my hand by the time I count to three or I'm taking you down."

"Hell, yeah!" His jubilant cry accompanied a suggestive swivel of his hips.

"One." Rylan took a little step back. He followed her. "Two." Not waiting, Rylan slammed her fist between the kid's eyes. The bridge of his nose crunched beneath the pressure. Her left knee rocketed into his balls, and he screamed, releasing her. Rylan shoved him as he scrambled to grab his nose and his groin at the same time. He fell backward into the crowd of bodies that bucked to get out his way like a school of terrified fish.

Her heart rate hadn't even kicked up. Rylan looked at the kid, not a single ounce of fear inside her. She was steeled, in control, and it felt damn good. The murmurs of the crowd turned into cheers and heckles, one voice breaking through.

"Hot damn. Well done, sweetheart."

Cole was reluctant to get any closer seeing how Rylan had one hell of a fist on her. He'd stood close enough that he could have intervened if she'd needed it, but hell love her, she hadn't. The sneer she gave him now was more unsettling than her brilliant show of super-cop powers. He deserved it.

Rylan tried to push past him, but he turned just enough to stop her. "What are you doing here, Cole?"

"We need to talk."

"I seem to recall you mumbling something when I met you, about not even being able to have a drink without work interrupting you. I think I know how you felt." She grabbed her purse, dug out her keys, and plowed her way past him this time. Cole lightly touched her arm. She jerked away, very clear danger on her face. This don't-mess-with-me side of her was impressive and made him all the sorrier for being an asshole.

"Tucker rode with me and drove your truck back with the spare key."

Her head whipped to the side, her eyes throwing daggers. "So, you're forcing me to stay here and talk to you?"

He shrugged. "Yeah, I guess so."

Rylan crossed her arms. At least she'd put her fist away, for now. "You have a great way of forcing people to do what you want them to, don't you?"

"Dammit, Rylan, that's not fair." He deserved her anger, but it was still hard to process. The disappointment and uncertainty in her expression hurt. "I'm leaving tomorrow for the mountain, and I don't want this hanging between us."

"I trusted you."

"You can still trust me, Rylan. I swear… When I made that deal with Livy, I'd never even considered that it was going to hurt anyone. I was terrified of feeling what you feel over Rachel. Having her ripped away from me… God, Rylan, I know I didn't handle it the best way, but I couldn't lose her."

The crowd was mingling around instead of dispersing the way he'd hoped. He'd been to this bar enough times to know how the crowd loved to latch onto anything juicy—a bar fight, a lover's spat, drunk women taking their bras off. Pissed-off ex-cops breaking frat boys' noses. Rylan fell silent, and it flagged his concern. He knew she probably hated him a little bit right now for mixing her past with the present.

"Rylan."

She shook her head and made her way to the door, pushing it open with both hands and stepping out onto the sidewalk. Cole followed, her continued silence killing him.

"Don't shut me out, dammit."

"Does it matter?" She rubbed her neck with a hand.

"Yes, it matters. Stand up to me. Tell me what you feel." He wiped a palm over his mouth and took a step closer when she sneered at him.

"Stand up. To. Me."

Her hands flew in the air above her head. "I can't!"

He grabbed her then, his fingers curling into the firm flesh of her upper arms. She jerked at the contact, her hands coming up to try to peel his grip away.

"You can. Yell at me. Tell me I was wrong! You can stand up to me, Rylan."

"I can't because I would have done the same thing." Her

voice growled into his ear. "I had to ask myself, if I'd had enough money or influence to make Peter hightail it out of our lives, would I have? The answer is yes, I would have, just to keep Rachel with me."

Cole let his hands fall down her arms, her words grounding him. Carefully, he pulled Rylan in until she rested stiffly against him. He embraced her; she didn't hold him back.

"I'm going to make it right. For Livy and Birdie." He could feel her tension ease away with the words. Cole pressed his face to her hair, willing her to soften in his arms. "I don't want to be the type of man that does the wrong thing, Rylan. I was just so desperate to keep her. And right now, I'm pretty desperate to keep you, too."

She melted into him then, her hands sliding up his back and crossing over his ribs. Then she was on tiptoe, pulling his head down for a desperate kiss.

"Let's go." He pulled her into the truck he'd parked just outside the door and drove like a bat out of hell away from town, out to the quiet country road that led home.

Rylan gripped his right hand in both of hers, sitting so close her hip and thigh burned into his, very nearly robbing him of all ability to concentrate on the road. Her thumbs stroked the top of his hand and his palm in tandem, drowning him in sweet, sweet electricity. Cole wished she'd say more, but took her touch and proximity for the forgiveness they were.

Rylan released one of her hands, her palm covering the top of his thigh. Even in the dim light, Cole could see the flash of silver in her eyes and the soft, sensual smile on her lips. Her hand slid up, her fingers digging into his inner thigh right before her nails raked slowly over his jeans. A sudden, blasting heat covered his cock when she cupped him, pressing hard against his rigid flesh.

"Jesus, Rylan." She massaged him, her thumb still tickling his palm, and it was nothing short of a miracle that he didn't crash the truck. He cut the normal twenty-two-minute drive from town down to eighteen, pulled in behind the house, and came to a stop. They were both out of the truck in two seconds flat, inside the house and tiptoeing like naughty teenagers to his room. Cole ushered her inside, locked the door, and was grabbed, two hands on his shirt, pulling him to the bed before he even had a chance to turn on the light.

Chapter Nineteen

Cole was much easier to push onto the bed than she'd figured. He was being easy on her, but it didn't matter. When he lay back, his arms crossing behind his head with a willing expression on his face, Rylan had him exactly how she wanted him. It really didn't matter how he'd gotten there.

He scooted back so she could straddle his waist and slip the shirt over his head. Her fingers found the hard, cut lines of his chest and abdomen. With a wicked smile, she moved down his thighs and smoothed a palm between his legs. Cole groaned but lay still, even when she worked the buttons and zipper of his jeans, opening the waistband down. He kicked off his boots as she pulled the denim away, throwing the jeans somewhere when they finally cleared his long legs.

Without warning, she placed her hands on the tops of his thighs and leaned low, taking him in her mouth in one hot slide. Cole's hands wound in her hair, his hips shifting up in surprise. Trying to ignore her own blazing desire, Rylan clenched her thighs and focused on the texture of him and the deep sounds of his pleasure. She licked him up and down, used her lips to pull his cock from base to tip. Small beads of moisture formed at the tip, and Rylan whisked them away with her tongue, her hand cupping his balls.

A sharp gasp was his reply as Rylan moved her mouth faster, pressed him harder with her lips. She grabbed his hip with one hand, holding his cock steady with the other while riding him with her mouth. Cole cried out and grabbed her softly beneath the jaw to pull her up.

"Ry, I'm going to…no, no, no, not like this!" He sat, gripped her under the arms, and pulled her up the length of his body. Rylan shrieked at the sudden power of the move and found herself flat on her back.

His taste was potent and heady on her lips, and she craved more. Her body thrummed with need for him, the constantly building ache between her legs making her thighs clench to hold back. She splayed her fingers through the soft, black hair covering his chest, weaving through it with soft strokes until the tight, hard lines of his abdomen met her. His body was a perfect composition of strong muscles, beautifully curved bone and soft skin. Touching him was a gift, one she would hold dear for the rest of her life.

Cole brushed his mouth across hers, stopping to tease the corner of her mouth with a little kiss before brushing to the other side to do the same. She smiled under the soft ministration, tipping her chin to take his lips when he pressed in for a deeper, openmouthed kiss. One hand slid to her belly, smoothing the fabric of her nightshirt over her quivering skin. His fingers shifted lower, teasing her with the promise of a touch where she wanted him the most. His palm whispered over her curls, making her hips jerk, before his hand worked back up and wiggled her shirt up over her belly, her ribs, her breasts. Each movement of fabric and flesh on flesh left a cold trail that was quickly replaced by Cole's heat.

He broke the kiss just long enough to whip the shirt off her body, his mouth stroking sweet pleasure from hers as she lay back down. His fingers raked down from the top of her scalp, letting big handfuls of her hair slide through his fingers. Shivers burst into desperation. Rylan grabbed his wrists, her legs parting wide. Cole gripped her shoulders before running his hands to cup her breasts. When he teased her nipples in tandem, Rylan shook her head and pushed her palms against his ribs.

"Don't make me wait."

Cole chuckled, moving one knee between her legs, followed by the other. His hips lowered and rocked back a little. Rylan ran her hands over the rippled muscles in his arms and glanced down at the same time he pressed the length of his erection against her sex. Heat permeated her folds, burning against her demanding clit.

"Jesus!" She grabbed his waist and dug her nails into his hard flesh as her hips tipped up and allowed his length to run straight down her center. Cole made a greedy sound, pressed his lips for an equally greedy kiss. She whimpered, curled her fingers around his firm ass. So needy…

Rylan turned her head slightly to break the seal of their lips. "I need you in me, now!" He grabbed her gaze. The heat and tenderness in his eyes stabbed straight through her, welling up to clench her heart as he nudged her thighs farther apart and slid into her in one long thrust. All the air left her in a rush and a loud moan.

"Shh… We're not outside this time, sweetheart."

Rylan bit her lower lip. When Cole slid his fingers between their bodies and found her nub and rubbed it with just the right motion, just the right pressure, she nearly suffocated from holding her voice back.

Then he moved. Slow, slick, each withdrawal and every slide back in forcing her body into a fast climb. She was surrounded by it, saturated in mind-twirling sensation until her clit and her brain threatened to implode. Her orgasm forced the clog from her throat, and there was no quieting the cry that shattered with her body. Cole buried his face against her cheek with a deep, primal groan while he followed her in release. Rylan wrapped her arms around his neck, her legs clinging tightly to his hips. They lay there for long minutes, breathing hard, pulses racing.

His comforting weight relaxed on top of her, his fingers strumming through the ends of her hair. She shifted beneath him. Cole groaned and flipped to his back, then reached over to turn on the bedside lamp. Soft light showed just how tired, and incredibly sexy, he was. He reached to the floor, producing a pair of sweatpants and a T-shirt, and tossed her the shirt. He slid into the sweats, slowly, much to her enjoyment. The longer it took Cole to cover up that amazing body, the better. The shirt smelled like laundry soap and Cole when she pulled it over her head.

He turned the light back off and pulled her possessively against him as they settled into the bed. Rylan turned in his arms until his breath washed over her lips. She marveled at the sculpted strength of his arms as they held her. Would she ever get used to this feeling? His hair curled up just a bit as she ran her fingers through it. As comfortable as this was, she knew he had to be up early, and that getting caught in his bed was the last thing either of them wanted. Rylan eased out of his arms.

"What are you doing?" he mumbled.

"I should go."

One strong arm braced across her middle. "Stay. Let me hold you." Despite how she warmed at that, she hesitated.

"What if someone finds out?"

He pulled a piece of hair away from her face. "Then I'll explain that it's perfectly acceptable for me to be in bed with the woman I love."

Rylan's body went cold, a hum starting low in her ears. "What?" Her pulse kicked up. He kissed the corner of her mouth, then the middle, and then the other side, soft words punctuating each kiss.

"I. Love. You." Cole smoothed his hand down her arm to her hand and wound their fingers together. Rylan searched his eyes in the dim light as shock squeezed hard and then let go. The moment took on a rightness that left her lighter, freer than she'd felt in longer than she could recall. It was the type of feeling she'd been hoping for. It felt like a second chance, and she wasn't going to hold back or overthink it. She wasn't going to let it slip away.

"I love you, too." Her lips tingled as the words tumbled out. There was no hesitation, just the truth she felt down to the deepest part of herself. She expected to find peace through hard work at Paint River, not in the arms of a man who completed her in a way she didn't know was possible.

"I'll take that over just blowing off steam any day, sweetheart." Cole's kiss scorched her to her very toes. "I'm burning that damn handbook when I get back. Sound good?"

She snuggled back against him. "Handbook?"

He pulled the covers over them. "You never read your employee handbook, did you, Rylan?" Cole yawned, and she followed suit.

"No."

He settled her against his chest, comforting her with the strong embrace of arms she'd never get tired of. "Good girl."

· · ·

Rylan woke to streams of new daylight filtering in Cole's open window and a bundle of something warm and soft pressed against her chest. Cole's long body was wrapped around hers, his face pressed against her back. She blinked slowly, reveling in the sensation of waking up next to him. It felt so right.

She stretched her arms, bumping the pillow or whatever was pressed against her other side. It stirred and yawned. Rylan shrieked. Birdie lay in a little ball on top of the covers. Her bottom was pressed against Rylan's chest, blond hair spilling over her shoulder. Cole shifted behind her, giving Rylan the sudden impression of being a sandwich. Trapped between the two people she longed to make her own.

Cole hitched up on an elbow and looked over her shoulder.

"Would you look at that?" His soft voice was pleased. "Little Birdie."

"Bed-hopping again." Rylan smoothed Birdie's hair away so she wouldn't pull it between their bodies.

"Always," Cole lamented with a yawn. "This saves me

some trouble. Wake her up."

It was barely 6:00 a.m., too early to wake a five-year-old who would likely refuse to nap later. Cole sat on the side of the bed and threw on a shirt. He tossed Rylan a robe with a wink. As she wiggled into it, Cole came around the bed and picked Birdie up.

"Wake up, baby. Let's show Ry our surprise." Cole jostled the little girl gently, and she blossomed awake against his shoulder. "Daddy and Tuck have to leave soon, so come on now. Wake up, sleepyhead."

Grabbing a small afghan to cover Birdie, they went outside into the shiny, crisp new day. Still groggy from great sex and deep, comfortable sleep, Rylan took in a big breath of cool mountain air and felt her soul expand. When Cole stopped beside the old herb garden, her soul almost burst.

"See!" Birdie squealed, wiggling to get out of Cole's arms. "They's pretty!" Three scraggly rosebushes filled the space, four pale-pink rose heads dropping under their own weight. A little sign sat in the middle of the plot, spelled in big, hand-carved letters. Rachel Roses. Someone—Birdie with Cole's help, Rylan guessed—used a black marker to put an apostrophe and an *S* at the end of Rachel

"I ordered some wood chips from the mill, and they had these in the greenhouse. Rachel tea roses, they're called. It's late in the year, but we'll mulch them good…"

Rylan threw herself at Cole, and he grabbed her with greedy arms, lifting her onto his waist as she hugged him hard. He petted her hair while his lips murmured his love, and Rylan wanted to die from the pressure in her chest. She didn't deserve this, any of this, yet she loved it so much.

Birdie pulled on the edge of Rylan's robe. "They're for

your little girl. So we remember her." Cole grabbed Bird-ie with one arm and lifted her up, too. Rylan squealed and laughed, sure he'd fall from their combined weight. But he didn't. He held them tightly while Rylan looped an arm around Birdie and kissed her hair.

"I don't know how to thank you for this," she said, a tear falling down her cheek.

Cole pulled her in for a kiss. "Sweetheart, you already have."

Chapter Twenty

Storm clouds reflected up from the water of Paint River, hiding the beauty of the stones as the men crossed the water. Cole called to Tucker that he'd catch up, watching a moment as the group of eight rode ahead. The men loved going up into the mountains. Cole usually did, too, but this time was different.

There was a woman at the ranch he couldn't wait to get back to. Rylan fit. Rylan was part of Paint River Ranch through and through. She had this country in her soul and a lifetime of farming in her to back it up. Marrying the judge and living in the city had taken away some of her down-home shine, but she'd get it back. Cole remembered the first time he'd watched her taking in the mountains and breathing the clean air. She'd transformed right in front of him from a woman who'd lost her way into a woman who belonged here.

He wanted to do everything he could to make this work

between them. He turned his horse to the left and walked into a shadow cast by the Wishing Tree. *Sometimes, you just need a little help to get what you want.*

Feeling equal parts stupid and hopeful, Cole reached into his pocket and took out a small gold ring. It was dull with age, but the tiny ruby in the center still shone brightly. It was his great-grandma McBannon's wedding ring. Maeve had given it to him when he'd asked for Livy's hand, and Cole was never as glad that he hadn't given it to her as he was now. Livy had demanded a shiny new ring. But this one, worn by history and the good hands of love, would be perfect for Rylan. Cole could already picture it on her slender finger, could see it glinting in the light. All he had to do was convince her that he and Birdie could be everything she needed. Making a wish wouldn't do any harm, he supposed. If Rylan believed the universe could help them out, he was all for it.

He took one of Birdie's curly pink hair ribbons out of his pocket and tied the ring to one end. Lifting up in the stirrups, Cole reached for the perfect branch and tied the ribbon to it. The little ring swung back and forth, bumping into a neighboring baby shoe.

"All right, tree." Cole looked around to make sure no one was near. "I wish for Rylan to be part of my family, with Birdie and me. If you can help with that… And I'm talking to a tree." He tapped the ring, watching it sway. "If you can help with that, I'd be much obliged." Cole tipped his hat to the tree and raced to catch up with Tucker, all feelings of stupidity gone. He just hoped it would work.

• • •

The wind picked up with a ferocity that reminded Rylan of tornado season back home. Maeve said it wasn't uncommon for storms to kick in hard and heavy, but even this was a bit unusual. No rain, no snow, just wind and lots of it.

Mother Nature meant business when she ripped all the sheets off the line and sent them flying. Rylan peeked out the side window to see the fabric whip across the yard. Birdie was coloring on the couch, the television softly spouting *Sesame Street*. Worry flickered through Rylan's mind. If it was this windy on the low ground, what was it like in the mountains where Cole and the cowboys were? They'd been gone two days, and Rylan couldn't deny how much she wished they'd return.

The only good thing about the weather was that it kept Birdie inside. The little scamp had tried twice to "find daddy" by wandering off. Birdie had tried following Cole during the fall roundup last year, too, apparently. She'd made it to the edge of the property, calling for Cole, before Maeve had found her. Rylan would keep a careful eye on Birdie while Maeve rested. At least the overcast sky and foul wind had them tucked neatly together and buttoned up. She and Birdie made peanut butter cookies to give "Daddy and Uncle Tuck" when they got home, and they colored pictures to hang on the refrigerator.

Rylan was grateful for the joy she experienced spending time with Birdie. Every now and then, a small flicker of unease would creep in, but it was easy to push aside. All she had to do was replay Cole's whiskey voice telling her he loved her and everything felt exactly the way it should be. A bang against the French doors made her shriek. Rylan raced over to see that a chair had tipped over on the deck. A second laundry basket went tumbling by, tangled sheets racing after it, blown over from the side of the house. Knowing she couldn't let the laundry flip over the yard, Rylan cracked the doors and stepped out onto the deck. The wind wasn't too bad out here. She could run and grab the sheets and come right back in.

"What ya doin, Ry?" Birdie stepped out behind her, a little hand on her leg.

"Honey, you go sit with Grandma for a minute." Rylan started to usher Birdie back inside.

"She sleeping." With a sigh, Rylan offered Birdie her hand.

"We're going to grab the sheets and run back inside, okay?" Hand in hand, they went down the steps and into the front yard. Rylan was relieved to find the wind weaker on the ground. It came in big gusts, pushing at them with an insistent hand before receding, only to gust again a few seconds later. They raced after the baskets and flapping linens, and picked up a few odds and ends left lying in the yard. Rylan was just about to lead Birdie to the porch when she saw the chickens. Everywhere.

The gate must have broken again. Hens ran willy-nilly over the gravel drive, some being pushed by the wind, others deciding to lie down and wait it out. With most of the ranch hands gone with Cole and Tucker, Rylan figured she'd just shoo them back into the coop herself. It wouldn't be the first time.

She and Birdie wedged the laundry basket between two chairs on the porch and trotted to the fowl. They startled easily, some following her, others running farther away. The wind died a little as Birdie held the gate to the coop closed so the chickens they'd managed to wrangle couldn't come back out. The noise of mad chickens mixed with the snorts of an angry horse and barking dogs.

"I'm going to get a scoop of feed. Hold the gate tight," Rylan called to Birdie, who did as she was told. Rylan stepped inside the little shed next to the coop and dished up some feed. When she stepped back out, the remaining loose flock was waiting for her. They jumped after the seed like ninja chickens, pecking and flapping at each other.

"Ha! Open the door, Birdie. Here they come—" Rylan looked up from leading the chickens to see the gate flapping and Birdie gone.

Her stomach bottomed out.

A piercing squeal followed by a *thwapt*. Someone shouted, a pissed-off dog howled. Rylan's hair clip came undone, her hair blowing wildly around her face as she raced toward the sound. Another high-pitched squeal—a terrified horse. The small corral near the chicken coop came into view, a blur of black-and-white racing around as Pana Bar Noir whirled and reared inside. The horse bucked, spinning in a tight circle, and a ranch hand came running from the barn, waving his arms and shouting.

Rylan's eyes went everywhere, searching. The little bump on the dirt inside the corral would have been unrecognizable save for the spill of bright blond hair. Rylan didn't think, she didn't feel. She ran, her legs pumping onto the solid ground, body doing a home-plate slide under the fence rail. Rylan cupped Birdie with her body, glancing long enough to see the puddle of blood around Birdie's head. *No, no, no!*

The little girl's back rose and fell, and Rylan sobbed with relief. She covered Birdie's body with her own on instinct as

Pana raced around the small enclosure, tossing his head in a wicked frenzy. Before she had a chance to think about how to move Birdie outside the fence, Pana charged her. Rylan saw two black hooves cut through the air, coming down right before she ducked her head under her arms. Two anvils on her back, heavy and sharp and crushing the breath from her lungs. Scissors cut flesh and bone, stealing her air and stabbing her throat with cold thrusts. *Can't breathe. Can't breathe.*

A gunshot rang out and the wind faded away. Rylan blinked, a red film squiggling across her field of vision. She blinked again and tried to move her head. The world was still—quiet, cold. And then it went black.

• • •

In the space of time between darkness and remembering, Rylan experienced two concrete thoughts: the universe was pulling a fast one on her and she heard a fiddle playing. All other thoughts had raced around in bits and pieces. Memories of Rachel, the farm back home, Cole's smile. The way his fingers felt on the small of her back. Birdie's giggle. Then, suddenly, the racing thoughts had moved like a storm cloud, revealing a crystalline expanse of pain. And the reality that Birdie was in danger of losing her life.

For the past twelve hours, Rylan had been trying to figure out how to deal with that pain, both physical and emotional. She'd sat by Birdie's bed, refusing to go back to her own room despite the pain she was in, the little girl's hand in her own. Maeve and Jim Gilfoyle interacted with the doctors as they came and went. Maeve's gentle voice was muddled in

Rylan's ears when she said a few men from a neighboring ranch went up in the mountains on all-terrain vehicles. They'd tried contacting Cole and Tucker on handheld radios but the weather ran interference.

Waiting was the norm in this painful new reality.

Birdie's head was heavily wrapped, leaving only a vertical strip of skin exposing her eyes, nose, and mouth. Wires and intravenous tubes were connected to monitors that blipped and beeped in steady rhythm. Rylan had a fractured memory of what happened—seeing Birdie on the ground, watching the stallion thrash his feet above her head right before a ranch hand shot him with rubber bullets to drive him off. Frenzied bouncing in a vehicle, the sounds of her own voice begging Birdie to wake up.

After being kicked in the head, Birdie's brain had begun to swell. While Rylan had been x-rayed and medicated for broken ribs, Birdie had gone into surgery to relieve the pressure, her skull drilled and tubes inserted to drain the extra fluid. Tears lodged in Rylan's throat, but she wouldn't let them grow. Guilt pressed down on her, suffocating and stagnant. She'd left Birdie to go chasing chickens. If she'd never gone in the shed…

"How are you feeling, Rylan?" Maeve slipped into a chair next to her. Rylan closed her eyes, never losing the rhythm of her thumb caressing Birdie's palm. Maeve put a hand on her shoulder, and the touch was tender and warm.

"I'm fine." Rylan's left foot bounced uncontrollably, sending shocks of pain through her broken side. Looking at Birdie, so fragile and helpless, was replaying moments Rylan wanted so much to change. She'd lied to Cole. She'd told him she would keep Birdie safe while he was gone, but she'd failed. For the second time in her life, she'd failed a child.

"Rylan." Maeve leaned in close and searched her face. "There is no blame here."

No blame? If she'd stayed inside, Birdie never would have thought the ranch hand trying to get Pana into the barn was Cole and run out into the corral. If Rylan had left the chicken tornado alone, Birdie would be running around Paint River in a pink tutu right now.

Rylan wanted to dispute Maeve's admission aloud, but the fight inside her was gone. "Thanks," she managed. Maeve shifted in her chair, and Rylan looked up.

"Maeve?"

"Yes?"

The room wavered, the noise in the hall suddenly hushed and still. "I love her so much—" The words sobbed out of her in a gush. "I told him I couldn't be a mother. I...I told him." Maeve's arms wrapped around Rylan's head, and she let herself be held, rocked. Like a child. Like a broken woman.

"I do love her. I swear I do. But I can't be her mom. Look what happened. Look what I did." Mumbles, grunts, maybe they were words—Rylan wasn't sure what was coming out of her mouth. Maeve didn't speak, and Rylan's guilt grew. She should be comforting Maeve, not the other way around. Jesus, she'd almost robbed Maeve of her only grandchild. Maybe still would.

A loud shout in the hallway and the sound of stomping boots broke their embrace. Rylan tried to straighten in the chair, but her broken ribs had other plans. Cole burst into the room just as she managed to sit. The cry that ripped out of him was filled with so much agony Rylan closed her eyes to pretend it wasn't happening. She'd run through this moment a million times in her head, trying to prepare for Cole's reaction. But there was no way to ever be ready for the raw emotion on his face.

He stood just inside the doorway, arms and legs frozen in a wide stance. His head was tipped low, the brim of his hat barely revealing his eyes. When he looked at her, his pupils rose to the very top of his eyelids, giving him a wild, crazed expression. His eyes were dark, dangerous, and so filled with grief Rylan didn't know how to begin to process it.

He took two steps and stopped. His eyes darted from Maeve to Birdie, then to Rylan with an ominous flare. Maeve rushed to him for an embrace, but Cole batted her away. Rylan quivered under his hard, unfailing gaze.

"What happened?" His voice was a low rattle. "Rylan, what happened?" His hat went flying, his hands raking into his hair. "You said you'd watch her!"

Rylan's skin froze to her bones. Her lips couldn't part to allow words to filter out. Cole broke through his stupor and rushed to the bed, kneeling and gently taking Birdie's hand. A sob ripped from him, once, twice. Cole touched the bandages on the side of her head, traced her small lips with one finger. He dipped his head.

"Daddy's here, baby. It's gonna be all right... It's gonna be — " His hands were shaking as though a small earthquake raced through his body. Cole let his hands drop. Rylan was sure her lungs had caved in or her broken ribs spread to the entire architecture of her chest. Even taking a slow breath was torture.

She sucked in enough air to whisper, "Chickens... I went out to get the chickens..."

His eyes clenched, hands fisting. "You left Birdie for… for chickens?" He rubbed a shaky hand over his eyes. "Jesus," he growled. "You told me you couldn't love her, but I didn't listen. I didn't *listen*."

The pain in her side was excruciating, but the stab of his words gutted her. "Cole—"

"You need to go." He slapped the arm of her chair. Rylan cried out as the vibration rippled up her side and through every ragged end of her bones. Gasping and stunned, she struggled to stand. Cole buried his head in Birdie's side, her small pale hand like a fallen leaf in his darkened, rough palm. Tears filled Rylan's eyes, blinding the path to the door as she shuffled out. She should stay and fight. She should wrestle Cole's pain and win. But she couldn't because she didn't deserve it.

Maeve moved to stop her, but Rylan shook her head. Cole's broken voice sounded from inside the room. "Birdie… Oh, baby."

"I'm sorry." Rylan palmed the wall, feeling her way in the hall through a curtain of tears. Tucker and Jaxon rushed to grab her elbows, but Rylan shook them off.

"Rylan, where are you going?" Jaxon's soft voice cut through her misery. "The doctor hasn't released you yet."

Cole gave an agonized shout from inside the room, and something crashed. Tucker swore under his breath and raced to Birdie's room. A moment later, Rylan heard the thud of two big bodies coming together, and Cole's soul-shattering cry. Her knees went weak, and she slipped to the floor. Her fault. All her fault.

"I've got you." Jaxon's arms slipped around her.

"Drive me to the ranch, please."

Jaxon opened his mouth to protest, his huge eyes shimmery and sad. He nodded and helped her into a wheelchair. "Anything for a hero. That's what you are, Rylan, through and through."

Chapter Twenty-One

Birdie took forty-eight hours and fifteen minutes to finally open her eyes. When she curled her thin fingers around Cole's hand, he felt the way he had the first time he'd held her—awed, dumbstruck, and so very, very thankful that she was healthy and alive.

He struggled with Rylan's role in what happened. Tucker and Maeve had tried to talk to him about it, but he'd kept pushing them off. He wasn't ready to hear it, didn't want to know Rylan's excuses. All the times she'd told him that she couldn't be a mother again ripped him from the inside out. She wouldn't have let harm come to Birdie on purpose, but what if she wasn't as ready to be with them as he'd thought?

Cole watched Birdie sleeping, the beeping of her heart monitor lulling him into a daze. Rylan had been hurt, too. Broken ribs, Maeve had told him, though he'd cut her off before she could explain how. Cole pinched the bridge of his nose, trying not to think about the woman he'd come to love so much being hurt or how she was connected to what happened to Birdie.

"Hey, bro." Tucker gripped Cole's shoulder. "I'm headed home. You need anything?" He slid a white Styrofoam cup into Cole's hand.

Cole shook his head. "No. Thanks."

Tucker hunched by the bed and trailed a finger over Birdie's sleep-pinked cheek. "See you soon, honey." He turned to Cole, his voice low as he flicked a toothpick between his lips.

"You haven't even asked about Rylan."

A wallop of guilt hit him in the chest. "Nope." Cole dismissed it, putting a hand on the chair handle to get up. Truth was his gut twisted like a cyclone at the thought that she'd been hurt. But she'd been well enough to go back to Paint River, and that was good enough for now.

Tucker shook his head with a disbelieving snarl. Cole stood and left the room, making it just outside the door before Tucker grabbed his wrist. Cole's face went hot.

"Don't, Tuck."

Tucker jerked Cole close. "She broke two ribs, you asshole! She threw herself on top of Birdie and got stomped on by that raging lunatic of a stallion of yours!" Hands landed on Cole's chest with a resounding slap as Tuck pushed him back against the doorframe. "Wake the fuck up! She loves that little girl, and she loves you, though hell knows you don't deserve it."

Cole grabbed Tucker's wrists and spun him. The veins on the sides of Cole's neck throbbed violently.

"What?" he hissed. Tucker swiped his arms wide, breaking Cole's grip.

"If Rylan hadn't thrown herself on Birdie, Birdie would be dead." Tucker's voice was hard and even. "And if Pana had hit Rylan a few inches higher, he would have severed her spine and *she* would be dead."

I took down a rapist and got a bullet.

She'd saved Birdie and taken a bullet, from the horse and from him. "But, she… She let Birdie wander off." He felt like sinking, wished the floor would open and swallow him into hell.

"She took Birdie with her to chase the chickens back in the coop. Birdie saw John with Pana and ran to the corral, probably thinking John was you. He couldn't get your stupid horse to cooperate and had gone in for some grain. Before he or Rylan could get to Birdie, Pana kicked her."

Cole looked up, bells ringing between his ears. "What?" The blood rushed from his head. He leaned against the wall as a flitter of dizziness passed. He'd automatically suspected the worst. He hadn't even given Rylan, or anyone, a chance to explain.

I took a bullet.

For the first time during the whole ordeal, tears blurred his vision. Cole thrust a finger at Tucker, his lips twisted with an anger he couldn't fully explain. Like a puff of smoke, it wafted away, floating out of him. Rylan put the life back in him, and now he'd likely sucked the happiness she was trying so hard to find out of her.

Tucker grabbed him in a crushing embrace. "You can make it right, big brother."

Hell, what had he done?

• • •

Rylan struggled into a pair of yoga pants, careful not to bump her ribs. The pain was better today, but if she moved just so, her body reminded her that she'd lost the horse-versus-human rumble. She'd been on bed rest for all it was worth, feeling miserable and useless. Today, though, Maeve brought the news that Birdie would make a full recovery, and Rylan felt she could breathe for the first time in two days, if only in a figurative sense. Physical breathing still hurt like hell. Now if there was a way she could face Cole, her heart might start beating properly.

She just didn't know if she wanted to.

She inched to the laundry room, cringing to see the un-attended pile. It took great effort, but she got a load started and another out of the dryer. Her body ached, and Rylan quickly realized that being out of bed wasn't that great after all. She'd thought being active would help the doubt that wouldn't leave her alone. She took a quick look out the laundry room window. The sky was overcast, the mountains dark. Like her mood and the thoughts swirling around in her mind. Like the decision she was pretty sure she was making.

Maeve stopped her with a shout. "Oh no! No working!"

"I'm fine, Maeve. I can't just lie around." A stab of pain through her ribs reminded her she should be doing exactly that.

Maeve leaned against the doorframe, legs crossed at the ankles. She raked her teeth over her lower lip for a moment. "Rylan, you saved my granddaughter. Saying 'thank you' doesn't seem nearly enough."

Rylan bristled and let the basket in her hands fall to the ground. "No, my actions almost killed her." Their eyes caught and held. Rylan put both hands on the dryer and bent her upper body low to ease the pain shooting through her side. Maeve walked over, put a warm hand on top of hers.

"I have so much to thank you for. For helping me. For making Cole happy again."

Rylan groaned and placed her forehead against the cool metal of the dryer top.

Maeve sighed. "I'm not blind. I know he's in love with you, Rylan. He's not very objective where Birdie is concerned, and he didn't handle what happened very well—"

"I wouldn't have expected him to." Rylan stood a little straighter, immediately regretting it and leaning back down.

"He'll make it right, Rylan."

Making it right with her probably wasn't the best idea. The way she'd let him down was something she had to work on, not him. He had every right to be angry with her. She should have taken Birdie into the shed with her instead of trusting her to stay put.

"I'm just not sure that I can…that I want… Maeve, I need a break."

She'd found purpose and new life at Paint River, but it didn't mean anything without the people she'd come to love. She'd finally started to make peace with Rachel's memory and let the painful bits of her past fade away. Everything inside was screaming that she protect that progress, even if it meant walking away until she could figure out what to do next.

"Rylan," Maeve whispered, her voice shaky, "letting my son and Birdie into your heart… I know that's really something, Ry. I do." Their eyes met and Rylan saw nothing but respect and understanding reflected back at her.

Her lower lip trembled as a small space of silence

stretched between them. Swallowing hard, Rylan gathered up her courage. Maeve gave a sad whisper of a sigh, the sound forcing Rylan's tears to fall. The universe was testing her, fine. It was also giving her the opportunity to do something about it.

It was time to leave Paint River.

"Maeve…I quit."

• • •

Time was something Cole was used to ruling with an iron hand. Up before sunrise, get everything on his mental list accomplished for the day, get home for supper. Read to Birdie. Go to bed. Now, the tick of the clock sounded a little maniacal and mocking. Each minute he spent away from Rylan was time wasted not trying to make up to her for his stupidity.

He'd never felt so torn between two people in his life — Rylan or Birdie — and was going crazy knowing they both needed him, though for completely different reasons. As the day ticked away with Birdie's hand in his own, Cole thought of all the things he should have done differently. And of all the ways he wanted to kick his own ass for being such a fuckhead.

When Birdie slipped into an afternoon nap, Cole left her in care of the hospital staff and raced home. All thoughts of what he was going to say fled as the pure need to *just get there* became almost overwhelming. Rylan would probably be in bed, nursing her broken ribs, maybe trying to relax in the tub. Maybe she'd be sleeping and he could quietly wake her with apologetic kisses.

Parking in the rear of the house, Cole wrenched the

back door open and raced into the hallway that led to Rylan's room. He grabbed the doorframe of her bedroom to keep from crashing in too fast and losing it. Chest heaving, he thundered inside. His legs went weak. The silence in the room knocked the wind out of him. He gripped the white metal footboard to keep from sinking to the floor.

The room was empty.

Cole closed his eyes against the rush of pain in his head. It slithered down the back of his neck and built a mansion inside his chest. He flung open the bedroom closet, looked under the bed and inside the dresser drawers. All empty.

Jesus, she was gone.

"Rylan!" His voice ripped out of him, part sob and part demand. He sank onto the edge of the mattress and rubbed his forehead with both hands. He should have done things so differently—been honest with himself about Livy earlier, faced his guilt instead of trying to ignore it. He should have learned the entire story about Birdie's accident before he took his anger out on Rylan. Could he fix this?

Cole looked up through a haze of foreign tears, a flash of red pulling his gaze. Beneath the small end table beside the bed, Rylan's red boots sat neat and tidy. A letter lay folded on the end table, next to a stack of smaller envelopes. He thumbed through the stack. Her paychecks. Numb, Cole opened the letter addressed to him and Birdie.

Birdie, I have no doubt you'll be an amazing woman one day. I'm honored to have known you and hope your daddy will put these checks into your college fund so you can live your dreams. I know that you will.

All my love,

Rylan

He counted the checks. They were all there, every single one since the day she'd started. He saw between the lines so easily. Birdie could live the life Rachel never had the chance to. In her own small way, Rylan was making sure Rachel's lost potential lived on through his daughter.

And he had doubted her.

A soft shuffle drew his attention to the door. He stood, hopeful. But Maeve walked inside, her face blanching when she looked at him. Cole rubbed his eyes.

"She left," Maeve said in a voice rich with sympathy. Sympathy he didn't deserve.

"Where did she go?"

Maeve frowned. "Jaxon drove her to the airport. Beyond that, she didn't say, and I didn't ask. I'm sorry, Cole."

He shook his head, struggling to get a grip. The clench in his middle and the out-of-control panic in his brain were extensions of what he'd experienced when he had learned about Birdie's accident. Birdie would be fine, but Rylan was gone.

"Don't be. This is my fault." He wanted to lean against something, sure his legs were going to give out.

Maeve's soft voice made unease well in his stomach. "I told her, when she was ready, to come back home."

Cole gripped the bed frame. A good eight feet separated him from Maeve, but Cole swore she'd just body slammed him. *Home.* Cole thought about the judge and how that life had sucked the breath out of Rylan. He didn't want to be that man. He wanted to be the man who made her feel alive. The way she did for him.

Keeping Birdie so close, she should have suffocated, and afraid of getting hurt and used, he'd shut himself out of life. Until Rylan. Through her eyes, he saw the beauty of Paint River again. Through her struggle to hoist herself out of her past, he remembered what it was like to let someone in. He loved her, and this was her home. He just hoped it wasn't too late to convince her of that.

"How long ago did she leave?"

Maeve smiled. "Half hour or so."

No more mistrust, no more second-guessing. He was awake now, eyes wide open. He kissed Maeve before racing from the room, grabbed his cell, and dialed Jaxon's number.

Chapter Twenty-Two

Rylan took a long drink from her water bottle to soothe the ache in her throat. She wasn't going to cry, dammit. Her brother's brief phone call to announce the arrival of his daughter, Kathu Rachel VanZecht, added a sweet layer to the knots of emotions pumping though her. That he and Trey had honored her daughter's memory by using Rachel's name for their own was more than she could even comprehend. Their father was hopping a plane to Australia tonight to go meet his new granddaughter, and Rylan wished she could join him. As it was, the trip from Missoula to Milwaukee was going to be rough with the amount of pain she was in. No way could she sit on a plane for twenty hours.

She gave Jaxon a wan smile, glad the ranch hand had offered to take her to the airport. He'd taken a phone call himself while she was talking to her brother, and now that they were both off, an awkward silence ensued. He didn't attempt conversation, and she was grateful. Anything he said right now would probably result in her breaking down in tears. They weren't even halfway to Missoula yet, and she didn't want to spend the rest of the drive like a sobbing idiot. She'd do that after he dropped her off at the airport.

Jaxon eyeballed her, and she gave a small smile, mentally willing him to keep quiet. *Don't bring up Cole. Don't bring up Cole.*

Cole. It hurt so much to leave him, but it hurt more to think about facing him. She couldn't bear the disappointment and pain she'd caused, and she didn't want to see that blank look in his eyes that he'd had at the hospital. Jaxon slowed down a little as she glanced out the window and watched where the skyline rippled as mountains undulated up and down. The scenery was bittersweet. Paint River had given her warmth a thousand times stronger than the cold of her pain had been. Rylan glanced at her hands—they were calloused. She'd never been one to have soft hands, but they looked different to her somehow now. In a short span of time, her hands had worked harder than they ever had, they had held and tended a child she'd come to love, and done all the necessary tasks of managing a family and a home. They'd traced a man's body and held him tight in passion. They'd wiped away blood and tears.

These weren't the restless hands of the judge's wife. They didn't hold a gun anymore, but they held memories. Everything she'd touched had touched her in return. Wasn't that the point? Setting foot on the ranch had given her the first full breaths of life she'd experienced in months. She'd let her fears rest by loving, by accepting, by standing up for herself, and by letting go. Now, she was waking to the possibilities for her future. In return for taking that leap, the universe had given her Cole and Birdie.

The truck rocked and stuttered a little. Jaxon eased it over to the side, limping along. He frowned and finally stopped.

"Huh. Something's up," he said as he unbuckled his seat belt. "I'm going to check it out." He popped the hood and slipped out of the truck. A seesawing ache nagged her side every time she tried to take a deep breath, but it still wasn't worse than the agony she felt over Birdie.

Birdie had danced and skipped right into her personal space and made herself at home. Five-year-olds in tutus did not always do what they were told, like holding the chicken coop gate closed and staying put. Five-year-olds had accidents like falling out of bed, and sometimes worse.

Jaxon's form came and went as he fiddled under the truck's hood. Rylan focused on his movements while her brain processed, for the millionth time, the fact that Birdie may well have found another way to try to find Cole. It didn't take away the responsibility she assumed for what happened, but it did hit home the fact that sometimes accidents happen.

Jax came around and leaned into the open driver's door. His violet eyes narrowed as he pushed back his hat and glanced around. "Ah, truck's broken down." He cleared his throat and moved away before she could ask what was wrong.

"What?" She pressed her head against her window while a wave of pain rippled through her side. Figures the truck would break down. On a long stretch of road that cut between mountain and plain without another ranch or house in sight.

Jaxon was on the phone, his head down, a foot kicking gravel on the edge of the road. After fifteen minutes of watching him fiddle around, she needed air. Rylan cracked open the door, gripping the frame tightly as she turned and slid her legs out. The simple movements hurt her ribs so bad, stars turned to fireworks behind her clenched eyes, blocking her senses beyond anything but agony. Something warm slid over her chilled fingers where they gripped the doorframe. The familiar feel and texture of the touch would have brought her to her knees if she'd been standing.

"Looks like you need a ride, sweetheart…again."

She couldn't open her eyes as the whiskey voice spiraled around her. She was afraid of what she'd see looking back at her. Cole's hands cupped her shoulders as he knelt down to where she sat on the edge of the seat.

"How can I apologize?"

His broken voice lifted the sob from her throat. Rylan looked into eyes mirroring her tears. Her hands shook. "Cole, how can *I* ever, *ever* apologize to you?"

"Come home." His shoulders jerked like he was going to embrace her, but he held back. Instead, his long fingers kneaded her shoulders while the rugged lines of his face turned pleading. "Love me, and Birdie, enough to come home."

Rylan exhaled, then groaned in response to the pain. Cole touched her face, his muscles tensing. She wanted to cry, to let the pressure out before her chest exploded. She gasped a breath and reached for him. Cole leaned in, gripping her under the chin, and kissed her lightly, almost as though he was afraid of hurting her.

"I do love you," she whispered against his lips.

Thick with emotion, his voice wavered. "I love you too, sweetheart." He embraced her lightly, and it was enough. It was perfection. Cole mumbled something, nuzzled her hair and trailed his lips across her temple to her cheek and hovered over her lips. He swept a tear from her lips with his thumb before placing a tender kiss there.

"The truck's not really broken down, is it?" Rylan asked with a suspicious grin.

He paused and kissed her neck. "Ah, no." Then his lips touched her jaw, the corner of her mouth.

She pinched his biceps with playful anger. "Cole Haywood!" He chuckled lightly against her lips before pulling her in deep.

"Just keep kissing me, sweetheart. Just keep kissing me."

Epilogue

The horse pranced as Cole maneuvered him beneath the Wishing Tree. Rylan clenched Cole's soft, warm shirt in her fingers, her knuckles pressed against his firm sides. The movement of the horse didn't hurt her ribs as much as she'd anticipated. Though she still had healing to do, the threat of a little pain wasn't enough to keep her from taking this moment alone with Cole.

Birdie had come home last week after two weeks in the hospital. She had to wear a protective helmet to prevent further injury until her brain had time to heal. That she'd come away otherwise unscathed was a blessing Rylan focused on to help salve her guilt over what happened. Cole had been amazing, splitting his time between caring for Birdie and caring for her. He took a break from overseeing every detail of the ranch to do so, handing off some responsibility to Tucker and Jaxon to help with the load. They talked, a lot. About the ranch, about the future, about silly things, and it was perfect. He decided to take little steps with Livy, introducing her slowly to Birdie until Birdie was old enough to decide how much she wanted Livy in her life.

Despite the change and constant worry over Birdie, Cole was more relaxed than Rylan had ever seen him, taking all the time he had to spend with them both. Knitting them together like the family she'd come to see them as.

Cole stretched up in the stirrups. "Here it is." He reached high in the branch. "You know, I owe you an apology."

Rylan hugged him as firmly as her muscles would allow. "Oh, really?"

Cole turned his head to look at her. "For a lot of things, actually." She touched his back and kissed his neck.

"But to start, I'm sorry for telling you wishes were stupid." Cole threw a leg over the saddle horn and jumped down. Rylan looked at him with a questioning smile while he turned away and fiddled with something. When he turned back, his face was serious with the slightest hint of amusement.

"You know, I hear Paint River has an opening for something you're very well qualified for."

She smiled, intrigued by the intensity in his eyes. "Yeah? What's that?"

Her brain refused to process anything beyond the love in his eyes, the love that held her so completely. He took her left hand. Rylan's jaw dropped when he slipped a beautiful gold ring with a ruby center on her finger.

He gave her the most intensely loving look of her life. "Being my wife." Rylan slipped off the horse into his arms. "I don't deserve it, Rylan, but I'm hoping you will see the best in me. You *are* the best of me. I don't want to be a replacement in your life, but an addition. An extension of the new life you're making."

An extension is exactly what she had in mind. There could never be a replacement for Rachel or the life she'd had before. Those memories would never be erased, but she'd learned to manage the pain. Cole and Birdie, this place, were everything she needed to fully let life happen again.

His finger traced softly along her spine. "Oh, Mr. Haywood, I believe you're coming on to me."

He kissed her senseless. "You're damn right I am."

Acknowledgments

It's really amazing how many people were involved in bringing this book to life. Behind these words is a supportive network of people who were just as excited (maybe more so) to see Cole and Rylan in publication. To my children, Jared, Hannah, and Andie, and husband, Matt, thanks for understanding the time it takes to bring a book together and for supporting me in my dream. There really are no words to properly thank you. I hope this shows you that you're never too old to chase, and catch, a childhood dream.

To the Mistresses of Rocking in Corners, thank you! Tamara, Tristina, Carrie, Angela, Heather, and Amber, you cheered me on the whole way from the minute I said, "What if you got off the bus in the wrong town?" and a story took shape. You're the best critique partners a girl can have, and I'm blessed that you chose me to be part of your group! To my beta readers and the WrAHM group, double thanks for your support (huge thanks to Gennifer Albin for forming such a fabulous group of women writers). I'm still humbled that my agent, Nalini, and editors, Danielle and Guillian, saw enough of what they liked in this story to take it on and make it better. Thanks, ladies! I'm so proud to be part of the Entangled family, and I hope this is just one of many books to come.

About the Author

Elizabeth Otto grew up in a Wisconsin town the size of a postage stamp where riding your horse to the grocery store and skinny dipping after school were perfectly acceptable. No surprise that she writes about small communities and country boys. She's the author of paranormal, and hot, emotional, contemporary romance, and has no guilt over frequently making her readers cry. When not writing, she works full time as a Emergency Medical Technician for a rural ambulance service. Elizabeth lives with her very own country boy and their three children in, shockingly, a small Midwestern town.

KEEP READING FOR A SNEAK PEEK TO THE SECOND BOOK IN THE PAINT RIVER RANCH SERIES BY ELIZABETH OTTO, ONE NIGHT WITH A COWBOY...

Chapter One

She was five minus two seconds from throwing up. Grabbing the sides of the whirling carnival-ride seat, Sophie Miller squeezed her eyes tight and dipped her head. How she let her eight-year-old nephew Ethan talk her into getting on this ride, she had no idea. A pile of puke in his lap was about to be the reward for his insistence.

Surrounded by tinny music, colorful flashing lights and the smell of heavenly fried food, Sophie had been glad they'd come to the street carnival. She loved the noise and the smells and the crowd. It was the perfect way to spend her first night back in Montana in six months, giving her the opportunity to catch up with her sister, Carla, and Ethan, while relieving a little of the stress that had plagued her for the past several months.

And then Ethan had talked her into getting on the Scrambler, and suddenly the carnival wasn't so fun.

A hard lump burned in her throat, and Sophie crossed

her hands over her mouth to hold back the nausea. Just when she thought she might lose it, the Scrambler began to slow down. The milling crowd swirled and faded below her only to reappear again as their cart went round and round a little more slowly each time.

She tried to focus, hoping it would keep her lunch firmly in her stomach. A tall, broad-shouldered cowboy in a white hat and light blue shirt stood out from the mass of people around them. The snippet of his face she could see as the cart whirled around became clearer on the next rotation when he looked up at her. A strong, square face and eyes that seemed to grab right a hold of her even in such a brief moment, and a long body with narrow hips making a drool-worthy contrast to his shoulders, was the most her brain could register before she swung around and lost sight of him again.

Mmm nice.

Since people-watching seemed to be helping her nausea, she was more than willing to keep eyeballing the cowboy. There he was once, twice, three times as she went around and around. Living in the city as long as she had, Sophie had no real experience with country boys, and this cowboy's rugged hotness reminded her she really needed to make up for that. A one-nighter with a guy like him to remind her of the pleasures of life? Yes, please. Sophie admonished the thought with a grin and an eye roll. That was the last thing she had time for right now, but as the thought skipped away, she realized her fear had, momentarily, lessened.

She found him in the crowd again, and then, as his image faded away once more, the ride stopped. Sophie's brain jostled inside her skull as she closed her eyes to try and find equilibrium.

"Coming, Aunt Sophie?" Ethan grabbed her fingers as he opened the cart door and jumped down.

She paused as the metal ride jiggled under the weight of its disembarking riders. Her entire world seemed unbalanced as the dizziness took hold, sort of like her life had been in general lately. The phone call she'd gotten from Carla three days ago, saying that their mother's health was declining had rocked Sophie more than losing her job four months ago had. While the deathtrap was definitely testing her resolve, Sophie knew this was one problem she could overcome.

Too bad standing right now seemed detrimental to her health and possibly everyone around her if her stomach let loose. She glanced around, looking for her hot-cowboy focal point, but he was gone. Disappointment shot through her. She'd hoped to catch a closer look on the ground, but no such luck.

With a determined frown, she stepped down and sighed to feel the solid ground beneath her feet. A group of kids raced past her to climb into the death machine next, and Sophie let out an amused breath. Twenty-nine and she still hadn't conquered motion sickness. The fact that she hadn't actually thrown up on Ethan, though, made her feel like maybe she finally was.

Take that, stomach! She mentally high-fived herself and unsteadily followed Ethan through the crowd. Ethan pulled her hand and urged her to walk faster. Sophie pulled back to rein him in a little—faster wasn't going to happen.

"There's my mom." He called out for her and waved to catch her attention. Sophie squinted, Ethan's slight form suddenly fuzzy like a blotchy oil painting. Sounds rushed her ears, lights from the overhead poles suddenly blinding. A cramp stabbed through her gut, making her dizzy. Six years of riding in the back of a speeding, bumping ambulance as a metro Paramedic, and she couldn't handle one silly carnival ride? There was something seriously wrong with that little twist of irony.

Sophie could make out her sister's form, and groaned, recognizing her sister's trademark impatience despite the distance between them. Carla waited near the mini donut truck, one hand on her hip.

Sophie gave Ethan a half-hearted wave. "Go ahead. Tell your mom I'll catch up. I just need to…" Ethan took off for his mom before she could finish. He knew better than to keep Carla waiting. Smart boy. Judging by Carla's stance, Sophie considered motion sickness a good trade for a few minutes away from her controlling sister. There was a reason she and Carla lived 1300 miles apart, and the few hours they'd been reunited reminded Sophie why. Cats and dogs had nothing on their sisterly relationship.

A twisting knot of pain made her middle clench. Sophie closed her eyes and took a deep breath, mindful of the people walking around her. She moved to the side where the crowd was thin, her foot catching on something hard and unyielding. Her body tilted backward, once again thrust into a quick motion that sent her brain into a tailspin. Firm hands caught under her arms just before her butt hit the ground.

Instead of the dirt-meet-posterior slam she was expecting, she was lowered down gently. Her left hand instinctively reached out, grabbing onto the nearest object for support. Denim. Warm, soft, well-worn denim. Before she could register any more, a haze of stars exploded behind her eyes.

A deep chuckle and silky voice floated down as she lay back on the ground.

"I'm used to women throwing themselves at me, but this was a little fast, don't you think?"

This was turning into a helluva good day. Tucker Haywood flipped a toothpick from one side of his mouth to the other. When his client wanted to meet here to let his kids run around while he and Tucker talked business, Tucker had initially resisted. It was a carnival—loud and crowded. Everything he hated. He'd rather stay at home at Paint River Ranch and hold the meeting in his office. But if going to the carnival meant selling a horse, he'd relent and collect a big, fat check for his trouble.

Now he had a beer in one hand and a pretty woman at his feet.

Go figure.

He'd noticed her on the ride, even chuckled at the horror on her face while the boy sitting next to her clapped and whooped as the contraption flew by. Tucker had almost walked away but then he noticed her eyes latching onto him. Not just once but each time the ride went 'round. Something about the stubborn, albeit nauseated, expression on her face made him hang around until she got off the ride. He wasn't looking for a woman tonight, but it had been a while since he'd had a little female company, even if it was just a drink and a laugh.

Noticing how green she looked just now, Tucker figured he'd be lucky to get that far. A white tube-top dress clung to full breasts and a narrow waist, the hem stopping just above toned legs with golden skin that shone in the overhead light. A yellow string peeking out beneath the fabric to tie around her neck promised a rocking bikini underneath. Light freckles dotted a straight nose and heart-shaped face he could picture cupping between his hands. She was pretty, even with her eyes clenched tight and her full lips pinched white. It might be worth possibly getting puked on to find out a little more — especially if there was a bikini involved.

Tucker hunkered down next to her on one knee. "Hey, I was just kidding. You all right?"

She grimaced. "I'm dying."

Tucker grinned. "You're not dying." He nudged her arm with his hand. The ride next to them dotted her hair and dress with bright polka dots of multi-colored lights. "Can I help you up?"

Her arm moved slightly to show snappy blue eyes with long black lashes. Her eyes widened. "Are you crazy? I'm dying here!" Warmth spread through him when her eyes locked with his. A twinkle of good humor flashed behind the misery in her gaze, and the left side of her mouth tugged up in what might have been a smile trying to bloom.

He tipped his hat back and shrugged. "It was just a ride."

She pulled her arm away from her face and pushed up on her elbows. Color seeped back into her skin. Thank goodness. But just when he thought she was on her way to recovery, a sudden frown clenched her face and she lay back down.

"That ride is the devil. I need some Zofran." She flipped off the six-armed, silver Scrambler that swirled and zinged in a tangled mess of chairs and bodies. Tucker chuckled at the unexpected gesture. Dimples curved beautifully in her cheeks when she managed a small smile. He wanted to see more of her spunk and was tempted to rib her a little extra just to see it rile up.

"Hear that?" He tilted his head toward the ride where shrieks and giggles rang out. "I think those four year olds are laughing at you."

She groaned with a furious twist to her pretty lips. Well, look at that little hellcat, Tucker thought with an appreciative flutter in his belly. Yep, there it was. She riled up real nice, and dang if he didn't like the fire in her eyes.

"See how well you do in the hot seat, cowboy." She flicked her eyes toward the ride. "Go on."

Tucker reached a hand out and to his surprise, she took it. Her fingers were soft and warm, and she trembled as he carefully guided her up. His thumb swept the back of her knuckles, her skin silky, her nails daintily curved with white tips. Not the hands of a ranching woman, that's for sure.

"I'm smart enough not to get on a ride like that," he teased with a wink, watching her closely.

She pulled her hand away with a cock of her head, and smoothed the front of her dress. "Meaning?" she challenged, swallowing hard and picking grass from her shoulder-length hair. He noticed her hair was two-toned, the ends a few shades lighter than the rest, like they'd been dipped in light blond paint. He swept his gaze over the length of her, drinking in the bracelets dangling on her right wrist, the bright red polish on her toes, and the shiny little blue purse slung over her shoulder. Everything about her screamed city girl. Tourist, most likely. She was the complete opposite of the women he was usually attracted to, but it was there.

Attraction—pure and insistent.

He flicked his toothpick. City girl or not, she had his attention. All of it.

He smiled wide. "Meaning, I'm smarter than you, apparently."

Her arms crossed. "Are you smart enough to get lost before I punch your wise-ass mouth?" Humor lit her face and chased away the previous sourness.

Tucker raised his eyebrows. He liked spirited things for the most part: hard-to-handle horses, ornery cows, and the unpredictable Montana weather. It made life interesting and kept his restlessness in check. But spirited women? No, thanks. He preferred them soft and supple, easy to manage and easy to leave. But something about the sparks this fireball was setting off made his brain do a three-sixty. He never was one to back down from a challenge.

"Honey, anything you want to do with my mouth is fine by me," he drawled, giving her a sly smile.

She gave him a long, hard look before a slow smile made sexy dimples appear. He wanted to smooth his fingers along her face but he wasn't about to set off even more of that dynamite inside her. Not yet. There'd be a million and one ways to set off fireworks with a woman like her. Tucker bit down on the toothpick and reined in the thoughts making his blood hot. Something in the crowd caught her attention—a woman with a young boy stopped across the crowd and gave a wave. She gave an encouraging wave back, in the kind of way that said she'd catch up later. Interesting.

Turning back to him, her eyes darkened in the moment right before she broke eye contact. Her gaze roved over his chest and down his middle, pausing at his thighs before flicking back up to his face. Tucker heated under the intensity of her appraisal—not realizing he'd been holding his breath until his chest started to ache.

The woman couldn't handle a carnival ride but had no qualms giving him a blatant once-over. He was used to women looking his way—never had trouble finding a little company when the inclination arose. In the past few months, the female attention he usually craved left him unsatisfied and uninterested. Until right now. Damn, he'd been holed up at the ranch too long, and this silky, curvy, hot-tempered beauty had his interest by the balls, and then some.

"How about I buy you another drink?" she offered, tilting her head toward his beer. "That should keep your mouth busy for a while." She smoothed one hand over the back of her hair.

Oh, yeah. Coming to the carnival was definitely a good call.

Tucker put a hand to the small of her back. Sweet warmth met his fingers, driving him to draw his hand up the fabric of her dress to the bare skin of her shoulder blade. He paused for a fraction of a second to see if she'd shy away from his touch. She didn't.

Tucker leaned close to her ear. The curve of her neck was delicate and beautiful, her skin radiating heat mixed with notes of sugar and vanilla.

His voice dipped low. "And when that's gone? Then what?" he asked as he steered her away from the ride.

She leaned toward him, as if pulled by his touch or his voice—maybe, hopefully, both. A soft rise of goose bumps lit along her back, followed by a gentle shudder. The smile on her lips promised everything he told himself he wanted to avoid. No more one-night stands. No more messy, near-miss relationships. He was alone for a reason, though the sultry sapphire her eyes had become made him forget exactly why.

She leaned against his shoulder, the heat of her breath seeping through the fabric of his shirt and giving him a hard internal tremble. Her arm went around his waist, her fingers gently kneading his shirt and driving home what he wanted.

Her. Under him.

She smiled sweetly, gripping his shirt hard. "Don't worry, cowboy. I'm sure we'll think of something."